BIG RIG
Books

The Fifth Codex

Robert Bresloff

THE FIFTH CODEX

ROBERT BRESLOFF

An imprint of Gauthier Publications

Gauthier Publications
P.O. Box 806241
Saint Clair Shores, MI 48080
Attention Permissions Department

1st Edition
Printed in Brainerd, MN (September 2011)
Proudly printed and bound in the USA
www.EATaBOOK.com

Hungry Goat Press is an Imprint of Gauthier Publications
www.EATaBOOK.com
Cover design by Kelly Pulley

Library of Congress Control Number: 2011935518

For my daughter Melissa, without whose help and encouragement this book might not have been.

CHAPTER ONE

Found

It was a typical May morning in the Yucatan Peninsula. The sun had risen high enough above the clear blue waters of the Caribbean Sea to expose the quiet stone buildings of a long abandoned city, a lost civilization—a lost people.

Standing at the base of the broad gray staircase, Richard Woodson shaded his eyes from the glare of the sun as he studied the largest building at Tulum. El Castillo, the ancient Mayan temple, a temple that for centuries had stood majestically on the cliff overlooking the rocky shore below, and the long abandoned city. Woodson was the leader of the archeological team restoring some of the stone buildings at this ancient Mayan city. A Midwesterner who loved the Yucatan and a seasoned veteran of Mayan restorations, Woodson was an accomplished archeologist thought by some to be the best currently working in the region. He had been in the Yucatan since 1998 and had headed up restorations in most of the major archeological sites. Though small in stature, Woodson was well known in the region as the iron man of archeologists. After only a decade in the field, his discoveries and rediscoveries of lost Mayan artifacts had become legendary.

It was only seven a.m. and the archeological team was moving quickly about the ancient ruins of Tulum working to complete the restoration before the site was opened to the tourists. Woodson removed his dark leather hat, pulled a blue and white handkerchief from his pocket and wiped the sweat dripping from his forehead. Careful not to disturb his wire-rimmed eyeglasses, he continued to study the collection of gray rocks and mortar that made up the staircase that led to the square shaped temple above.

Woodson was somewhat disappointed to be on this project. Tulum, though the most popular ruins with the tourists that visit the Yucatan, was a Post Classic Mayan city that had been, even at its height in the twelfth century, little more than a trading post and a seaport. Still Woodson loved Tulum; especially with the large square temple, El Castillo, that looked down onto the Caribbean from high atop its rocky cliff. He loved the nature that existed there more than any site he had worked on in the region. But after three years in the Yucatan Peninsula he was actually looking forward to going back to his home in Chicago. When the university had requested his presence at this site, he'd thought, Why me? My apprentice, Pedro, could head this project. Most of the restoration work being done at Tulum was just small block replacement and adding palapas, or grass roofs, to some of the smaller buildings. This was done so that the tourists could get a feel for how the buildings might have looked nearly a thousand years ago.

As Woodson stood looking over this vast ruined city, he could hear Pedro, his sixteen-year old apprentice, calling his name. Pedro had been down the hill replacing some stones in a small building. He was a native Mayan and the grandson of Woodson's good friend, Angel, a well-known Mayan shaman or holy man. Since being assigned to Woodson's team for the summer, Pedro had become Woodson's friend and trusted assistant. Pedro stood well over five foot, tall for native Maya, and still appeared to be growing into his height. His grandfather, who Pedro had lived with since his parents had died in a horrible automobile crash, said he was clumsy. Woodson, being much closer to Pedro's age, understood the boy's awkward appearance. Dark skinned with thick curly black hair, pleasant features and a wide toothy smile, Pedro was a handsome young man that everyone on Woodson's team enjoyed having around. He studied archeology and Mesoamerican culture at the University at Mexico City and one day hoped to be an archeologist.

"Woody! I think you'd better come down here," he hollered.

Pedro had already slipped back inside the small gray building before Woodson could reach its small doorway. The doorways of most of the buildings in Tulum were only four to five feet in height. The Maya built their doorways so they would be forced to bow to the gods as they entered holy buildings. This building was obviously part of the temple complex. The building was tiny with two identical doorways directly across from one another. A small stone alter no more than a foot or so high, and just large enough for one person to sit on, stood in the very center. Woodson squeezed through the opening and dropped to his knees just next to Pedro who was seated on the small altar.

"I was getting ready to mortar this loose stone when it slipped and... it fell on my head, Woody!" Pedro removed his straw hat and rubbed the spot where the stone had landed.

"Are you okay?" asked Woodson. Though concerned about his young friend, he tried very hard not to smile.

"Yeah, I think so. But that's not why I called you, Woody. When I went to restore the stone like you told me to, I reached into the space to check for debris and I found something!"

"What did you find?"

"Look for yourself. I left it right where I found it!" Pedro leaned back allowing Woodson to look into the opening.

Woodson stood up and peered suspiciously into the dark opening left by the fallen stone. Though there wasn't much light coming into the tiny building, he could make out what resembled a long cylindrical jar. Woodson carefully removed the cylinder from its resting place and carried it outside into the light. There he began to inspect every inch of it with his magnifying glass. The jar was about fourteen inches long, approximately six in diameter. It appeared to be made from the clay used in this region for making pottery. But there was something about this jar that puzzled Woodson.

"This is amazing Pedro!" Woodson said as he reached into the building and pulled his apprentice, who was still rubbing his head, through the small opening. "This is codex pottery. Look at the symbols placed around the ends. Codex pottery glyphs were designed to tell a story or record a historical event. This one is different... unlike anything I've seen before. It's sealed as if there may be something inside. But this can't be. Archeologists cleared this place of all relics years ago."

Woodson turned it over to look at the bottom of the jar.

"Spanish? Pedro, look at this! Here just below the symbol of Chaac!" Chaac was the Mayan God that governed rain and agriculture.

Pedro took the cylinder from Woodson and inspected the area.

"How can there be Spanish on Mayan pottery?" he asked as he gently turned the cylinder in his hand.

"There it is! It's as plain as that bump on your head. It says Guerrero. We've got to open this cylinder! I've got to see what's inside! "

Pedro started to back away.

"Hold on Boss," he said, pointing at the cylinder. "Can we do that?" asked Pedro, concerned that they might be doing something very wrong. "Shouldn't we hand it over to the university? I think—"

"Oh come on, Pedro—where's your sense of adventure? No one but you and I know that we've found this thing." Woodson paused; he could see that young Pedro wasn't going to be easily convinced. "Look, the university will probably get all caught up in legalities; it could take months before they open it. The Mexican government has complete control here; they could hold up the opening for months. Besides we're just going to take a little peek. What's the harm in that? Then we'll turn it in. What do you say?"

Pedro leaned against the building.

"Uh...well, if you think its okay," he said uneasily, "I wouldn't mind seeing what's in there. You don't think that the Guerrero who left this is, the Guerrero?"

"Who else could it possibly be!" replied Woodson.

Pedro smiled with excitement.

"He is a legend, the first Spaniard to set foot on our land and to live among my people."

"Now you're talking Pedro. Put it in my backpack and we can open it when we get back to our rooms.

Now let's get back to work. The tourists will be piling in here in about three hours."

As Woodson and Pedro packed the cylinder into the bag, neither one noticed that they were being watched. Pedro pulled the bag up over his shoulders and squeezed back into the building where he had found the cylinder. As he replaced the block of stone that had fallen, his eye had caught movement just outside. He could feel that someone was watching—and not from far away. By the time he had reached the doorway to investigate, whoever it was had disappeared. All he could see were groups of workmen busily cleaning up around El Castillo.

After restoring the fallen stone, Pedro noticed that a round, bearded man dressed in bright white trousers and a straw hat had joined the group of workmen and was busily sweeping up some debris near the stairway to El Castillo. This was the first time that he had noticed this man since the restoration began. He thought it odd that he hadn't seen him before. Pedro made a mental note to ask Woodson later.

Pedro and Woodson sat quietly, staring at the artifact. Woodson gently picked up the cylinder and inspected the thin plate of clay that sealed the top. Silently he reached for his pocketknife, gently scraping away the years of mud and mold that secured the top to the cylinder. As he was about to break the seal he felt his shirt dampen from the sweat running down his back. What was in this cylinder? He thought as he watched the blade shake in his trembling hand. Will it be worth risking my career and my reputation? Was Pedro right, should I turn it over to university? Pedro reached out and grabbed his hand. Woodson jumped at the touch.

"What?" he gasped

"Not too clean Woody. Maybe if it looked like it fell off by accident it would be better."

"Good idea Pedro!" he replied, bringing his arm up to wiped the sweat from his brow. "I'll try to be careful." Woodson paused just before he brought the knife back to the top of the cylinder.

"Woody?" Pedro again interrupted Woodson from touching the seal with the knife.

"What now?" said Woodson impatiently.

"Who's the new guy I saw at the site today? That round guy with the beard. The one dressed in white. I don't remember seeing him before," replied Pedro.

"I don't recall hiring anybody that fits that description. What was he doing?"

"He was sweeping up around the steps at El Castillo. I'm not sure, but I think that he might have been watching us when we were looking at this," said Pedro, pointing at the cylinder.

"Hmmm... I think we'd better—" Then suddenly, the lid separated from the top of the cylinder and fell, spinning noisily as it hit the top of the table. An eerie silence filled the small room as it quickly spun to a stop. Woodson looked at Pedro in disbelief. Pedro's heart pounded so loudly each beat felt like an explosion going off in his chest. Woodson carefully turned the jar upside down. Slowly and without assistance a roll of brown colored paper-like material slid out from the cylinder just far enough for Woodson to grasp, and carefully remove. As the paper was nearly free of the cylinder, a string of green beads fell onto the table. Carefully, Woodson picked up the scroll in his left hand and the beads in his right. He handed the beads to Pedro. Cautiously, being careful not to tear it, Woodson opened the roll of paper, smiled and said softly, "It is most definitely the Guerrero."

How long have I been here? Are there any other survivors? I thought, as I felt the heat of the morning sun burn my exposed skin.

I looked up and down the white sandy beach. I could feel the sand on my face and the taste of brine in my mouth. How did this happen? How could we be so safe and secure on that gallant ship and only moments later be rowing for our lives? Yes the storm. I thought it had taken all hands but me until I stood up and saw nearly a score of bodies also moving about and probably having the same thoughts as I. First I could see my dear friend Geronimo then Juan and then in the distance they came. Savages—naked, savage, and they held long spears. Their bodies were painted blue and white. My head was still not right. It felt like a dream. The natives seemed friendly. They helped the men who could not walk and brought fresh water for all. Somehow, I am not sure how, they managed to make us understand that they were taking us to their village. It did not matter. We were so exhausted and some of the men were near death. We did not resist. At least we had been found! Little did I know that I would never again set foot in my beloved Spain! All I could think of was that these savages found us and that we were still alive.

Gonzalo Guerrero

As translated by R. Woodson

CHAPTER TWO

Escape

There were seventeen of us that were washed up on the shore. I do not have any idea where we were. We were quite certain that we did not find our way back to Cuba. The village that the savages brought us to was small but orderly. There seemed to be structure in this small society. The leaders treated us as guests but the villagers seemed to hold us up as Gods. All was good for a while. Our sick and injured men were treated by the savages as best they could. But still, three of our comrades died.

How long we were in this village I am not sure. The savages fed us twice a day. We ate flat bread and meat that tasted like pork followed by a thick, hot drink that was most enjoyable. Not only did this diet sustain us but it also made us strong. We were only allowed to walk about the village two at a time accompanied by an armed escort. At this point I realized that we were not guests but prisoners. The village was very small. Twenty buildings built around what we would call a square. The buildings were quite small and made from what looked like many stones with woven grass roofs. The children ran naked and played everywhere while the women, wearing colorful dresses covering them from neck to foot, worked at grinding some type of grain in large bowls that, I of course, now know to be maize.

I fully realized our plight when two of our comrades did not return from their walk in the village one day. That night there was a great commotion. Much chanting and what sounded like drums pounded loudly. I could not sleep that night. Somehow I knew what had happened to our comrades for we were no longer allowed to leave our huts.

After this night it seemed at every new moon two of our men would not return and the night would bring with it the same screams, chants and drums. Finally with only seven of us left, our captors decided that we had resigned ourselves to our fate and they let down their guard.

One night, before the next new moon we tricked the guard into thinking I was ill. When he knelt at my side I pummeled him with fists knocking him out cold. We ran from our prison as fast as we could, looking for anything we could find to help us in our escape. As we ran past the plaza we stopped in disbelief. The scene that lay before us was unimaginable. We found what was left of our comrades there. It was obvious the skeletons that hung by their feet were all that remained of them. I believed that they were murdered in some vile religious ceremony possibly ending in the consuming of their flesh. I knew we must escape at any cost.

In our escape we killed two, possibly three savages. My friend Brother Geronimo Aguilar, a sailor who fancied himself a man of the cloth, tried to stop the killings but the men were scared and frantic to escape. We managed to make it to the beach and made off with a large canoe. No savages gave chase and not one of us was injured. We drifted down the coast not knowing where we were headed but glad to no longer be where we had been.

Gonzalo Guerrero
As translated by R. Woodson

"Pedro, hand me that glass again will you? I can't seem to make this out." Woodson carefully poured over the ancient brown scroll spread out in front of him.

Pedro reached over and, with a questioning glance, handed him the magnifying glass.

"It seems that Guerrero and his comrades were the victims of a tribe of cannibals that existed in the Northern Yucatan," explained Woodson.

"Si, Woody. This we know, according to Bishop de Landa who documented all that went on during the Conquest," replied Pedro.

"I know Pedro, I know. But as I read this journal, I feel there is more to it than just a history lesson. There's got to be a reason why he would hide this thing in what, at that time, may have been an already abandoned city."

"No, no. My grandfather told me that Tulum was still occupied when the Conquistadors arrived. He's told me the stories of how the Maya bravely repelled the invaders." Pedro quickly replied.

Woodson looked thoughtfully at the papers.

"Maybe he was caught by the Spanish and wrote this while in captivity."

Pedro picked up one of the sheets.

"The rest of this isn't going to be easy to translate, Woody. Some is represented by glyphs and some is in Spanish."

"I know it's going to be tough, but with your help, I think we should be able to get it."

"My help!" gasped Pedro. "I just completed my first semester in glyphs!"

Woodson smiled at his young apprentice.

"In which you got straight A's… so you say." Then before Pedro could respond, "Now let's get some sleep. We have to be back at Tulum at six a.m."

The next morning, Woodson and Pedro joined the rest of the archeological team already at Tulum. Woodson gathered everyone at the steps of El Castillo.

"Okay, everybody, listen up," began Woodson, "I need Roberto and Julio over by entrance B where they bring the tourists in. Some of the rocks are coming loose and—"

"Woody!" interrupted Pedro, "Roberto isn't here."

"Who's seen Roberto?" Woodson quickly inquired of the workers.

The men just looked around at each other, shaking their heads and mumbling.

"There was a bearded man working here yesterday," said Pedro. "Does anybody know who he is?"

The workers responded the same as before.

Woodson gave the rest of the team their assignments. He then turned to Pedro.

"You'd better come with me. I think we might have a problem." They started toward the building where they had found the jar. Once inside, they saw the stone that had once hidden the cylinder, was now missing from the wall.

"That stone didn't grow legs and walk away on its own, Pedro! You replaced it yesterday. Someone's removed it!" Woodson examined the spot thoroughly.

"Who? The man I saw yesterday?" Pedro asked.

"Maybe... or maybe it was Roberto that you saw while replacing the stone! Funny that he's missing today. Isn't he the one who always had that red handkerchief sticking out of his back pocket? If he knew we already had the cylinder why would he move the stone?" Woodson stepped out into the sunlight. "I think we now have two mysteries on our hands, one in the past, and now another in the present."

CHAPTER THREE

Dzibilchaltún

We drifted for many days in that canoe. The men felt that we would surely die of thirst and hunger before we could find a place to land. We were more afraid now that we knew what these savages were capable of doing. Finally in desperation we landed our vessel in search of food and water.

We had found a cove near a beach and hid the canoe. We then headed inland. The land was a dense brush like jungle that seemed almost impenetrable. All around were large lizards. We were very hungry and wondered what the creatures might taste like. After sometime, the men had found what looked like a deep hole with water at the bottom. The climb down the rock wall was difficult but not impossible. At the bottom, we found caves to rest after we drank our fill of the fresh, cool water. The mood of the group improved as we made our way up out of the well to search for food. As we reached the surface, my senses picked up things moving about. Just as the last man emerged from the well I saw them come out from the jungle. I felt that this time all was lost. Wearing plumed headdresses, leather tunics and armed with great spears, these savages were no doubt fierce warriors.

After uneasy moments of being prodded and sniffed, our captors began touching our beards. They smiled with delight. They eagerly herded us onto a path that actually led to what resembled a road. These people built roads! I knew then that these were not the same people that had captured us before. As we were escorted down this road, made from stones that gleamed white as if bleached, some of the men began to cry and moan. I called for them to stop this behavior and show these savages no fear.

As we approached a clearing in the jungle we could hear a great commotion. I knew that the village was ahead but I had no idea of what I was about to see. As we came out of the trees we passed through a great wall that seemed to go on forever in both directions. We could see building after building, each one getting taller as we continued. I thought how incredible it was that these people could build cities. The men were awe struck and speechless. Our captors continued to look at and touch our beards and kept repeating the word "Kukulkán" in an extremely excited manner.

We were then led to what looked like a small pyramid and were taken up the very steep stairway. Some of the men nearly fell but we helped each other and all made it to the top where we were greeted by what I now know to be the High Priest of the city. He spoke very loudly and pointed toward the wall of the temple behind us. One by one we turned to view what the High Priest was pointing at only to be amazed at the sight before us. There on the wall was the likeness of a bearded European man. They thought that we were some kind of gods. As we looked down we could see people gathering to hear the High Priest speak. He spoke to his people as they stood in silence. I felt a sense of obedience to his authority. As

I looked out over the city I was amazed at how large and clean it was and how civilized the people seemed. It appeared to be as big as cities I had visited in Europe. The entire city was paved with stone. It was amazing how the buildings shone like polished glass and the roads gleamed white in the light of the blazing sun. I, of course, could not understand what the priest was saying but as he waved his arms toward the city as if it were a gesture of welcome. He smiled and said to us "Dzibilchaltún".

Gonzalo Guerrero
As translated by R. Woodson

As the morning work at Tulum ended, Woodson and Pedro headed back to their room to continue deciphering the mysterious journal.

"Woody, are you familiar with the legend that surrounds Guerrero?" inquired Pedro.

"Only that he was one of the first Spaniards to set foot on Mayan territory." Woodson stopped, and tipped his hat down over his glasses while he scratched the back of his head. "Let's see... that he lived with the Maya, married a native woman and had three children with her. All boys, right?"

Pedro nodded.

"Did you also know that he fought alongside the Maya against his own countrymen because of the deep love that he had for my people?"

"That I knew. But, I also heard that shortly after the Conquest began; he disappeared never to be heard from again. Is there more to the story Pedro?"

"Angel would tell me stories that he said were handed down since the beginning of time. So many stories, that I can only remember a very few. But I do remember the one about Guerrero. It's always stuck out in my mind, and I don't know why."

"What did Angel tell you about him?" Woodson asked as he opened the door, to the hotel lobby, for Pedro.

"Gracias. Angel spoke of how the Maya gave Guerrero the name, Halach uinic, the leader, because he spoke for his small group of men. His friend Geronimo Aguilar hated the Maya as much as Guerrero loved them. He vowed to escape at any cost. The Maya called Aguilar Ah Dzuudz or The Haggard One because of his deep despair

"In 1517, Guerrero led an ambush that defeated the first attempt by the Spaniards to invade, what is now, Campeche. The leader, Fernando Hernandez de Cordoba, was mortally wounded in the battle, but lived long enough to return to Cuba and tell untrue stories of Mayan cities made of gold and unimaginable riches. Aguilar was angered by what Guerrero had done. In his anger he left the city and was captured by another group of Maya.

"When Cortez landed on the island of Cozumel, he learned of Spaniards living with the Maya on the mainland. On hearing this news he sent a ship to the north to find them. The Conquistadors found Aguilar first, buying his freedom with green beads, probably very much like the ones we found in the cylinder. Then they set off to free Guerrero. Aguilar begged his friend to leave the Maya and join him in the journey to Cozumel. Guerrero knew it was too late for him. He loved the Maya and his new life. The story ended with Aguilar giving Guerrero the green beads that were meant to buy his freedom from the Maya."

"Green beads... hmmm... What of the other Spaniards that were shipwrecked with Guerrero?" asked Woodson.

"They had all died of loneliness or disease. Guerrero and Aguilar were the only ones that survived. Guerrero arranged for an escort of Mayan warriors to take Aguilar and the Conquistadors safely back to the ship that would take them to Cozumel. Guerrero stayed to live with the Maya. The legend says that Guerrero, his wife and children disappeared shortly after Aguilar left for Cozumel."

"What about Geronimo Aguilar? What became of

him?"

"He had learned enough of the Mayan language to act as an interpreter for Cortez during the conquest."

"Was there nothing more about Guerrero?"

Pedro and Woodson stopped in front of the door to the room.

"Only that he and his family went off to some lost city. A city that to this day has never been discovered. They say his family finally settled in Akumal. Some say that Guerrero lived there himself."

"You sure know your stuff about Guerrero," said Woodson. "How come you remember his story?"

Pedro shook his head. "I'm not sure, Woody. I've always felt... some kind of connection with him. Maybe that's why Angel loved to tell it so much."

"A connection to the past..." Woodson's voice trailed off as he slid the key into the lock. "You had me until that line about the lost city. You don't believe that stuff do you? Nobody has spent more time than I have looking for clues to a lost Mayan city. It's almost an obsession, I—"

Woodson opened the door to the room.

"What the—!" Woodson gasped. The room had been ransacked. The intruders had emptied the drawers and the closets, throwing all their clothes and belongings on the floor.

"It's a good thing we had the jar with us Pedro. I think you need to tell me a little bit more about this lost city!"

They went about the room picking up the mess. Not a word was spoken until Woodson spied something lying on the floor.

"Look familiar?" asked Woodson. "Doesn't our missing friend Roberto always have one of these sticking out of his pocket?" Pedro walked over and picked up the red handkerchief.

"Roberto did this?"

"Looks like it! He turns up missing today and now we find this! But who does he work for and how could they possibly know about what we've found?" Woodson held his hand up before Pedro could say a word. "I think we need to take a little road trip!"

"But Woody, I—"

"Never mind, let's get this place cleaned up and pack."

"I thought we were just going to open the jar, see what was inside, and then turn it over to the university," said Pedro, reminding Woodson of what they had spoke of the day before.

"Well things have changed. Something is really starting to smell bad, and I'm going to get to the bottom of it."

"Woody, you have to think this through, amigo. We can get into big, big trouble for what you're thinking about doing! What would Professor Lyons say?"

"I almost forgot about Lyons—"

"I don't think he'd be too happy with us!"

"I've got this feeling in my gut and I'm going with it. Don't worry about Professor Lyons; I'll let him know what I'm doing. I can't ask you to take the risk, Pedro, but I plan on deciphering this journal until I find out what this is all about. I'll understand if you want to pull out."

"Where to Woody?" said Pedro with a shrug and a smile. "Where you go, I go Boss!"

"Dzibilchaltún!"

Pedro's jaw dropped. "Why there? Shouldn't we finish deciphering Guerrero's writings first?"

"No time! Somebody knows that we have the journals—I'm not sure who it is—but it seems they want it pretty badly. We need to go where Guerrero began his relationship with the Maya. If this is where he learned of the lost city, then this is where we need to go! We can decipher as we go! Let's pack and head to Playa del Carmen. From there we should be able to book a flight. We can fly to Merida where we can rent a car. Did Angel teach you to drive?"

"Si. But Woody, the lost city is a legend. You said yourself that there's probably no such place."

Woodson grinned; his suntanned face sharply contrasted with his white teeth.

"Ah... but what if there is such a place? Someone else obviously knows about Guerrero's journal, or they wouldn't have ransacked our room looking for it.

We've got to get to the bottom of this. Get your things together, go to the front desk and tell them that we need a car."

"What about the work at Tulum? We can't just leave!"

"I'll contact Julio. He can handle what's left to do there."

"Do you think its okay for me to go with you, Woody?" asked the young man sheepishly.

"Don't worry; I'll call your grandfather. I'm sure he won't mind. Now go tell the clerk at the front desk that we need a car. Pronto!"

Thirty minutes later, Woodson headed down to the lobby of the hotel looking for his assistant. He stopped at the front desk.

"Excuse me, Señor, but was my assistant able to reserve a car?"

"Señor?" replied the small, plump man behind the desk.

"I'm sorry, a young man named Pedro," said Woodson, "He was supposed to tell you that I needed a car. It would have been about thirty minutes ago."

"Si!" replied the man with a smile as he pointed over Woodson's shoulder. "I remember... there he is Señor Woodson, out in front by the red car."

Woodson turned around to see young Pedro wearing a big smile, standing next to an old, beat up red Volkswagen convertible. He turned to the man and said, "That's all you've got? Will that thing even make it to Playa Del Carmen?"

"No problem, Señor Woodson," said the man behind the desk, "I have one just like it! Here let me help you with your bags."

CHAPTER FOUR

Aguilar

At first these natives must have thought of us as gods. We came to find out that, Kukulkán was the plumed serpent god represented by the image of a large bird gripping a snake in its talons. What was so amazing about this was the presence of what looked like a white bearded man along with these creatures in the stone carvings in the temples. As I grew to understand more of their language and customs I came to a very sketchy conclusion that this god gave them much knowledge and then disappeared into the sea. The Maya believed that he would someday return. As time went by, the Maya realized that even though we resembled these images we held no special powers. We were just men.

My companions and I were at this city for what seemed like years. As I look back, I remember the sorrow that they shared. They were all lonely for their families, friends and homes. After approximately two years they started to die one by one. Whether they were truly ill or died of loneliness I will never know. Only Aguilar and I had managed to survive. We were treated very well during this time. I learned to embrace this new life and learned to love these people. And as I began to understand more and more of the language and writings, the closer I became to the leaders. Their acceptance of me was remarkable. They gave me the name "Halach uinic" meaning "The Leader" because, before they died my companions looked to me for leadership. I enjoyed my time with the Maya. But my friend Geronimo, he did not. Aguilar hated these people and wanted only to leave this place. Nothing I did could convince him that he should make the best of the situation. The Maya called him "Ah Dzuudz" because of his haggard and unhappy appearance. Now that I think back on that time, he was. No matter what I did, he tried to undermine my efforts to understand and know these people better. I think that my friend began to hate me and probably

wished that I would die as well.

Gonzalo Guerrero
As translated by R. Woodson

The hallway was dark, but the silent figure found his way. The building was old and odors of dirt and spoiled food filled the damp hall. The figure stopped at an unmarked doorway. He knocked three times, as he had been instructed, and waited for a response.

"Enter," said the raspy voice from inside.

Slowly he turned the knob and pushed the door open; there he stood frozen in the doorway.

"Roberto?" the voice asked from somewhere inside the room.

"Si," answered the man in the doorway.

"Bueno! Come Roberto. I have been waiting."

The man entered carefully studying his surroundings. The room was very dark, like the hall, he was glad that it didn't smell. His eyes were growing accustomed to the darkness; he could barely see the small round figure that approached, passing quickly and closing the door.

"Well, where is Woodson taking the writings?" inquired the small round man, as he turned to look at Roberto.

"I do not know," answered Roberto, struggling with his English. "How is it you know my name?"

"I know many things. But never mind, you were to have had information on where Woodson was heading."

"The man who hired me said —"

"Fool! It was I who hired you!" interrupted the husky voice.

"No, it could not have been. The man was taller—with a beard!"

The small, round man walked over to a desk in the center of the room. He opened a drawer and pulled out a fake beard and a pair of shoes with lifts in the heels.

"I have to be a master of disguise, my friend. There are those who would very much like to see me disappear."

Roberto walked over and inspected the beard and shoes.

"You needed to trick me?" he asked. "Turn on the light so I can see you better!"

"With what's at stake, I trust no one. If you get a good look, you can recognize me. We can't have that, can we? Now! Where is Woodson?"

"On his way to Playa Del Carmen, that is all I know."

"We have to head him off. Woodson is very clever and he knows this region like the palm of his hand." The small man held out an envelope to Roberto. "Here! Take this. It should be enough to get you to the Playa. There is a car parked out back. The keys are in it. Check the glove box, you should find a little something

in there to persuade Mr. Woodson, if necessary. See if you can find them before they get any further. If I'm not mistaken Woodson is headed for the airport. There's a number to reach me in the envelope. Call me when you know anything. Did you hear me? Anything!"

Roberto stepped back and shook his head.

"Señor, I do not know what this is all about."

"Things you could not possibly understand. But for you, my friend—money—lots of money. Are you still interested?"

Roberto looked around the dark room trying not to make eye contact. Finally, he nodded his head.

"What about the boy? The archeologist has a young student with him."

"I don't care about anything but what is in that cylinder. Head for The Playa, find Woodson and see if he has the cylinder with him. This cylinder will have some ancient papers in them. I need to know if he has translated the contents. If he has, bring everything to me. Do you understand?"

"How will I know?"

"You must find him with the cylinder," snapped the raspy voice, "He will have a writing pad with notes on it. The notes will be in English. This is what I want you to bring to me."

Roberto grabbed the envelope and headed for the door. As he grasped the knob, in his sweaty hand, Roberto turned and asked, "Who are you Señor, por favor?"

The small man picked up the beard and held it up, and with an evil smile, answered softly.

"Call me... call me Aguilar. Now go, quickly, and do not fail!" he yelled as he dropped the beard into the open drawer.

CHAPTER FIVE

The Woman

After we had been at this place for some time- I am not exactly certain of how long because I was not familiar with the seasons. But from what I learned from the High Priest and his daughter, I have surmised that we had been in this new land about three years. It would be, I think, 1514 but I am not sure. These people are quite amazing. It seems that they have developed a calendar with a solar year of 360 days and that it is broken up by the spring and winter equinox very similar to our own. They are not savages, yet they have a lust for human sacrifice and many victims give themselves to it freely. They are not often held, but these sacrifices are a public event. There is much chanting and what seems like praying. They have many Gods. There is Chaac, the God of rain and planting. They seem to revere him the most. They seem to have gods for nearly every need or occurrence. However the one god that sends them into a horrible frenzy is the one they call Ah Chuy Kak, the God of sacrifice.

I cannot find the proper words to describe the things that I have seen. Let me say that these rituals are barbaric and inhuman. I have seen a living heart pulled from a man's breast and his lifeless body thrown down the steps to the court below. His skin was savagely ripped from his body and worn as bloody robes over the shoulders of a priest who danced wildly to appease the Gods. Children with their hands and feet bound thrown into cenote's, or wells, to drown. This is also done to appease the Gods. I will forever be haunted by the visions of these poor wretches as they faced their death. I can only hope that my death will bring me the peace that will blot these awful events from my mind.

By all that is holy I should hate these people. Brother Aguilar despises them and preaches to me to do the same. But I cannot find it in me to do so. In spite of the horrible things that occur here, these people fascinate me. Their way of life and their accomplishments are undeniably incredible. They have built cities that rival the best our civilization has to offer. They have a political system that is so strong that the decisions made at Dzibilchaltún, which means, The Place Where There Is Writing On Stone, can affect the surrounding area for miles in all directions. There are wonderful temples to tell the seasons and to worship the gods. The roads, they call them sacbé, are marvels in themselves. From what I have deciphered they connect the cities throughout the region. I have yet to learn of these distances, but from what I can tell, they must be great indeed. In my mind I can only compare the architecture to what I have read about the great pyramids in Egypt.

I think I am falling in love with the High Priest's daughter. She is called Zazhal ab. I believe it means The Dawn. I found her to be more beautiful than any sunrise. We have become very close. She was assigned to instruct me in the ways and language of the Maya. We spend many hours together by the order of her father, the high priest. She teaches me the spoken and written word of the Maya. She also teaches me of their legends. It was from her that I first learned of the lost city. She was taller than most of the other native women, though she would not be considered tall in Spain. Here the people are very tiny. I would say a good head shorter than the average height of a Spaniard. Her eyes are dark and crossed, which is considered the height of elegance. Her features with her flattened forehead, it is a common custom to flatten a newborn baby's forehead between two planks tightly lashed together, are a smoothness and softness that match her perfect brown skin. I think she may feel the same about me but it is quite hard to tell. If Zazhal ab decided to return my love I would be the happiest I have ever been. I was never really happy in Spain. I have no family or attachments to my home and I have never felt love before. This is why I came to the New World. Now for the first time in my life I think I feel happiness.

Gonzalo Guerrero

As translated by R. Woodson

"Here it is Pedro! Guerrero writes about the lost city!" exclaimed Woodson.

"You're kidding?" replied young Pedro.

"The lost city, Pedro, your lost city may exist! How much further to Playa del Carmen?"

"Ten, maybe fifteen, minutes."

"When you get to town, head for the Red Eye Café. We'd better get some food before we head to the airport."

"Si, Woody." Pedro sighed loudly.

"What's wrong?"

"The food there is all vegetarian. I could really go for—"

"Go!"

"Okay."

After some time, they arrived at the Red Eye Café, a small, quiet restaurant away from the touristy areas of the Playa, or hotel zone. The Red Eye Café attracts more of a bohemian, artsy type of crowd that keeps mostly to themselves. Woodson figured it would be the perfect place to stop and do a little more work on Guerrero's journal. No one would notice or even care what they were doing.

The Red Eye Café seemed dark after being in the bright afternoon sun, but their eyes adjusted quickly as they sat at the table furthest from the door. The smell of cooking oils and tequila hung in the air as they spread the papers onto the table.

"So you've read about my lost city?" Pedro joked, while Woodson unrolled the journals.

Woodson confessed that his excitement grew with every word of the journal that he read.

"This section is incredible, Pedro. He writes of his seduction by the Maya, and about the woman that he fell in love with. It's getting really interesting. I think Guerrero has left clues, not only in his writings, but probably at some of the sites as well."

"Does he describe the lost city?"

"He mentions it only briefly, but I think we're going to know more as we read on—"

Just at that moment, Woodson glanced up at the doorway. A dark figure entered the café. The bright sunlight that streamed in through the open doorway made it impossible to see who it was. Woodson was starting to get a little edgy about strangers and wanted to see who had come in. Then he noticed something very familiar about the way the person strolled into the bar. It was the walk. As the bright sunlight glared through the open doorway and surrounded the stranger's shape, there was no doubt in Woodson's mind that the stranger was a woman, and that she was walking right toward him. It was a walk Woodson would never forget.

"Blue? Is that you?" he asked, but the answer was never in doubt.

"Well if it isn't my old pal, Woody!" said the woman, as her features were now in plain view. "Of course it's me you big dope! What are you doing here in the Playa? I heard you were going back to Chicago!"

Woodson couldn't believe how good she looked. Her long brown hair and tanned skin made her beautiful large eyes look as blue as the Caribbean. Her real name was Marilynn Trotter, but because of those gorgeous eyes everybody called her Blue. She was only about five foot two inches tall but she carried herself with an air of authority. Blue was always in charge.

Woodson wasn't really sure how to greet her. They had met about three years earlier while working together on a small restoration project at Chichén Itzá. After a couple of months, their friendship gradually grew into a relationship. They had fallen in love. As time went on and their work separated them, their relationship began to cool. However Woodson still had deep feelings for Blue, and she knew it.

"Emergency restoration at Tulum, Blue," he joked, as he stood to gave her a big hug.

"What kind of emergency?" she asked playing along.

"You know, replace a stone here, and stick a little mortar there because the tourists don't understand what those ropes around the buildings mean." Woodson placed a hand on Pedro's shoulder. "You remember Angel's grandson, Pedro don't you?"

Blue grabbed Pedro's hand and shook it warmly.

"I can't believe it!" she exclaimed as she took a small step back to get a better look at Pedro. "You must be a foot taller since the last time I saw you. So what brings you to the Playacar, boys?" Blue then yelled over to the bartender, as they took their seats. "Hey Señor, dos tequilas por favor! Oh— bring the bottle and a couple of glasses."

"What about me?" cried Pedro.

"Oh yeah... and a Coke!" chided Blue

"You're driving Pedro," added Woodson with a smile.

"Nice outfit Woody, you still look like that Indiana Jones guy, although I think he had a better whip!" laughed Blue.

"Thanks a lot Blue," said Woodson, with more than a little impatience in his voice.

Before she said another word, Blue looked down and saw the writings spread over the small table. Being a skilled archeologist herself, Blue knew when she was in the presence of something important, wasting little time in getting right to the point.

"It is so good to see you, Blue. How long has it been?" Woodson asked, sensing Blue's interest in the material that was spread out on the table.

"Can it, Woody! What do we have here?"

"They're just some old papers, nothing important. How have you been?"

"I said cut the crap, and tell me what this jazz on

the table is all about!"

"Okay, okay, I knew you wouldn't fall for any hot air as soon as I saw the way you looked at this stuff," conceded Woodson.

"That's better," said Blue. "Now get on with it."

The bartender brought a bottle of tequila, two clay shot glasses and a tall coke to the table. Blue began to pour the tequila's.

"Woody! Do you think we should get Blue involved in this?" asked Pedro.

"Don't worry! You know Blue's okay. And besides, we may need her help. When it comes to archeology she's been around the block a few times."

Blue raised an eyebrow at Woodson's comment, and finished pouring the tequila.

Woodson and Pedro explained how they found the writings and the events that had brought them to Playa del Carmen. Finally when they were done with their explanation, Blue sat there, silently, staring down at the ancient documents.

"Who is this Roberto character?" she finally asked. "Do you know him?"

Woodson quickly shook his head.

"This was the first site that he had been with my team. I'm pretty sure that he's working for somebody who knows about this and wants it."

"Government? University maybe?" she inquired after downing her shot of tequila.

"Not sure, but he doesn't fit that mold. I think there is something else going on. I just can't put my finger on it," replied Woodson.

Just then, another figure appeared at the door. This time it was a man. He walked slowly toward their table. It was hard to make him out, with the sun still streaming through the doorway, but it looked like he was wearing something on his face. As he grew nearer, it soon became apparent that he was holding a gun and wore a red bandana covering his nose and mouth. Woodson signaled for Pedro and Blue to remain calm and stay seated, and slowly pushed himself up from his chair and leaned over the table.

"Can I help you, Roberto?"

"Que?" said the masked man, as he reached the table.

"It is Roberto, isn't it?" Woodson asked. Then he pulled an identical red bandana to the one the man wore on his face from his pocket, and threw it on the table. "I believe you dropped this when you were redecorating my room back at Tulum!"

Roberto was visibly trembling now and seemed confused. It was obvious to Woodson that their new friend had little or no experience in handling a gun. Glancing at the table, Roberto spied the writing tablet he was looking for.

"I will take that paper, Señor."

"I don't think so, Roberto. And put that gun down

before you hurt somebody," replied Woodson.

"The only one that's going to get hurt is you if you don't give me what I want." Roberto was shaking so badly, that he now held the gun with both hands.

Woodson started toward Roberto, as he did, he knocked the writing pad onto the floor. In the instant that the man's eyes glanced down, Woodson's fist came up and connected with the gunman's chin. With a thud, Roberto was sent reeling to the floor, his gun skidding loudly across the room. As he struggled to get up, Pedro grabbed the half filled tequila bottle and hit him over the head. The blow knocked Roberto out cold, sprawled out face down on the floor. Woodson walked over and picked up the gun and handed it to the bartender.

"Would you mind throwing this away?" He then turned to his companions, "I think that maybe it's time to head for the airport—before he wakes up," said Woodson pointing his thumb over his shoulder in the direction of where Roberto lay unconscious on the floor.

The trio gathered everything up and headed for the doorway.

"Nice work Pedro!" said Woodson as he stepped over the man's unconscious body.

"Gracias. You don't think I killed him, do you?" asked Pedro, his voice sounding a little shaky.

"Nah! I heard him moaning. I'm sure he'll be all right."

"Could somebody please tell me what that was all about?" demanded Blue. "That jerk had a gun. This is some serious stuff you've gotten into, Woody!"

"More serious than I thought. C'mon with us to the airport and we'll talk. Look, there's the car," he said as they stepped out into the street. "Get in!"

Blue stopped dead in her tracks.

"What is that?" she laughed.

"Our car, c'mon, get in," urged Woodson impatiently.

"Where? The back seat is full of your stuff—"

"Pedro, you drive. Blue, you sit on my lap! C'mon, hurry up! We don't know if Roberto is working alone. Get in the car!"

"Where did you say you were going?" inquired Blue, before she committed to getting into the car.

"Dzibilchaltún!" he exclaimed.

"Aw... what the heck!" she cried, squeezing into the tiny car and onto Woodson's lap, Blue put her arms around his neck and gave him a very hard, long kiss on the lips.

"Woody, it's really good to see you again." Blue reached over and mussed up Pedro's curly, jet-black hair, causing his dark young face to redden. "Okay Pedro," she cried, "Step on it!"

CHAPTER SIX

Another Enemy

As the years passed I could remember no time that I had ever been happier. I think three years had passed but I was still confused by the Mayan calendar. Zazhal ab became my wife and after a pilgrimage to the sacred island of, Cuzamil, to pay homage to Ixchel the goddess of fertility, she gave me three sons.

I remember the boys were still quite young, when the messenger came from the coast telling of the Man-Gods. I of course knew they were not gods—they were my countrymen. Aguilar was out of his mind with happiness upon hearing the news., He vowed to join them. Reluctantly, I had him held prisoner until I could fully assess the situation.

I convinced the leaders that these Man-Gods were not gods at all and were no more than Maya. They were just men!

The natives had seen the Spaniards atop their horses and thought that they were one god-like being.

I surmised that our enemy was Fernando Hernandez De Cordoba of Cuba. Only he could put together such an assault. Even when I was in Cuba, stories were told of how he was going to lead an army to this region to find his cities of gold and untold riches. I told the leaders that there was a way to defeat these invaders and that I would lead their warriors myself.

When I went to Aguilar to tell him what I was to do, he spat in my face. He screamed that I dare not do this and that I should reconsider my decision. I apologized for the grief that I had caused him. I also told him that I had no other choice but to keep him under guard until I returned.

The next day, with two hundred of the fiercest warriors, I left for the small Mayan coastal settlement of Ah Kin Pech. De Cordoba either knew what he was doing or was very fortunate indeed to have chosen this place to land. The few warriors that were in this small settlement were no match indeed for his well-trained Conquistadors.

Not knowing the land or its people he would never expect my small army of Mayan warriors, especially one that was led by another Spaniard. In his mind, I'm sure that the resistance that he had met at the settlement would probably be as difficult as he and his one hundred men would ever encounter.

We traveled by water for days in large dug-out canoes that held as many as forty men. We sailed just along the coast until we reached a small cape near an island. Our scouts told us that this place was the safest to leave our canoes. They were correct. If we had moved any further down the coast we would have been seen. We rested for the night without a fire. In the early morning as the sun began to rise and fill the sky with blue, we found their camp. The concept of flanking an enemy was not easy to explain to Mayan warriors. They only knew how to confront their enemy straight on. Somehow I was able to make them understand the strategy. We moved around the camp and surrounded them on three sides, leaving them only one escape. The sea!

It is so very hard to recollect what transpired during our attack. The Conquistadors had just awakened and we could smell their morning fires. Being so early, many of them were not yet wearing their armor. We took them completely by surprise. My warriors were fierce and efficient as they swooped down upon the unsuspecting invaders. The Maya seemed to enjoy the bloodletting immensely. They were not satisfied only to kill their enemies, but participated in mutilations I could not even dream of. De Cordoba himself was seriously wounded during the battle and was quickly taken back to his ship. Somehow I stopped the carnage so that the retreating Spaniards could escape. As the survivors rowed for their lives to the safety of their ship, I thought to myself that letting them live might have been a mistake. Later on I would come to know that it was! It was!

Gonzalo Guerrero

As translated by R. Woodson

"Blue. Are you going with us? I need to know now!" Woodson demanded loudly, as they stood at the ticket counter at the tiny airport in Playa del Carmen.

"You don't have to yell," replied Blue "My god this airport is so small!"

"The plane leaves in fifteen minutes. So if you could—"

"What in God's name are we going to Dzibilchaltún for, anyway?" snapped Blue.

"For your information, I am buying tickets for Chichén Itzá," replied Woodson.

"Chicken Pizza?" Blue threw her hands up. "What happened to Dzibilchaltún?"

"I think we might need some help, and Lyons is at Chicken Piz... I mean Chichén Itzá. Now you've got me doing it." Pedro started to laugh. Woodson just shook his head at them both. "Please stop calling Chichén Itzá by that silly name. You know that I hate that. Now—are you going?"

"Sure Woody, I would love to go to Chicken Pizza with you," she said, giving Pedro a quick wink.

Woodson bought the tickets and they walked outside to wait under the shade of the palapas for the next flight out. The afternoon was hot and breezy. The heat coming off the small runway that cut through the brush jungle was so intense it could take your breath away.

"Why don't we wait inside, where it's cool, Woody? How is Professor Lyons going to help us, anyway?" asked Blue.

"Remember our friend, Roberto? He may show up here at any time, and in case we need to get away, that little gate over there leads right into the city streets," said Woodson pointing at the small rustic doorway behind them. "And as far as Lyons is concerned, he's probably the most brilliant archeologist I have ever known. He might just be able to shed some light on this whole mess." Woodson shot Blue a stern glance. "Is that good enough?" he asked sarcastically.

"Geez, it's hot!" said Blue acting completely disinterested. Then she grabbed Woodson's hat from his head and began to fan herself with it. Just at that moment, she heard the sound of an airplane engine whining and sputtering as it made its approach toward the tiny runway. Blue looked up and shaded her eyes from the sun, "That, better not be our plane Woody!"

"Sure is, Blue! Ain't she a beauty?" Pedro quickly replied, as he shaded his eyes from the sun to watch the ancient, twin-engine plane touch down. It was an old prop puddle jumper used to move the tourists around the Yucatan.

"Oh my Goodness!" cried Blue as she sat down and dropped her head hopelessly into her hands. "It's got patches on the fuselage! I can't do this Woody! I tell you I just can't."

"What happened to the Blue I used to know? It's Pedro's first time and he's not scared!" said Woodson. "Right Pedro?"

"Uh—sure, Woody," replied Pedro with a degree of uncertainty,

Woodson motioned for Pedro to grab Blue's other arm and help her into the plane. Then, just before they stepped up into the rickety craft, Woodson could tell that Blue wasn't kidding. She truly was scared. Woodson turned her around and looked into her beautiful blue eyes,

"I would never let any harm come to you. You have to believe that!"

Blue looked deeply into Woodson's eyes, smiled, pulled her arms from his strong grip and jumped up into the plane unassisted.

"What are you waitin' for boys?" she cried, "You're holdin' up the show!"

Woodson and Pedro glanced at each other, smiled, and quickly followed her up the gangway and onto the plane. The take off went smoothly, but once they were clear of the city, the small plane traveling at only a few thousand feet began to jump and buck. The thermals, or pockets of heat, rising up from the jungle were the cause of the turbulence. The passengers remained fairly calm, even Blue. Pedro's nose was practically glued to the window. It was the first time that he had ever flown, and he was enjoying every second.

They spent most of the forty-minute flight translating Guerrero's message from the past. But this next section seemed to provide no further clues to the mystery.

"Well Pedro, what do you think?" inquired Woodson.

"This is amazing, Woody, I already know so much of this from the stories that Angel told me."

"Well, I hope, as we read on, we can get a better understanding for what this is all about. Quite frankly, I—" Woodson fell silent, once he realized what was coming into sight. The plane was preparing for the traditional circling of the incredible ruins of Chichén Itzá. As the plane banked over the ancient ruins he pointed out how the great pyramid, El Castillo, The Temple of Kukulkán, rose so majestically above the green jungle below.

Pedro's face was fast against the window. Woodson could see the awe in his bright young eyes as they reflected back in the glass. Looking away from the Pedro he turned to Blue.

"No matter how many times I take this flight I always get the chills when they circle the ruins." Woodson looked toward Pedro. "Take a look at Pedro. It reminds me of my first time." Woodson suddenly felt Blue's hand find his; a feeling that he missed. "After we see Lyons, and then Dzibilchaltún, I think we'd better go to Cozumel, Blue. I know someone there who can help us."

"Angel!" exclaimed the smiling Pedro.

"The one and only. I'm sure your grandfather will be able to shed some light on all this. Nobody knows Mayan history as well as Angel," he answered. "Look we're about to land. C'mon Blue don't be scared."

"What makes you think I'm scared Woody?" replied Blue softly.

"You're squeezing my hand so tight it's turning blue, Blue!"

"Oh! Sorry."

After arriving at the airport at Chichén Itzá, they rented a car and headed for the ruins. Chichén Itzá was the place where Woodson and Blue had first met. It was a quiet car ride to the ruins. Staring into the brush jungle as they sped along the narrow road, Woodson thought of the first time he met Blue. He also thought of what might have been.

"Pedro, head to the Mayaworld Hotel and park the car there," began Woodson. "We can get to El Castillo faster from there instead of the main entrance. Blue, I want you to book us a room at the hotel while Pedro and I look for, Professor Lyons."

Pedro pulled into a space next to a tour bus.

"Okay, everybody remember where we parked the car," said Woodson.

The afternoon was hot, and pesky, irritating insects buzzed around their heads. Woodson and Pedro headed into the jungle, toward the Temple of Kukulkán, the most magnificently restored step pyramid in the ancient world of the Maya. The temple, also known as El Castillo, is the largest and most imposing structure in this ancient city. Built to signal the equinox, the temple is situated in such a way that when the sun sets on the first day of spring, the large steps that make up the pyramid cast a shadow on the balustrade along the stairway, to form what appears to be an undulating slithering serpent. This pyramid was the second attempt to create the illusion. The first temple was built seventeen degrees off the mark. Armed with new calculations, the Maya built a new temple directly over the old one, hitting the coordinates exactly. Thousands of tourists gather every year at this site to witness this amazing phenomenon.

As they broke into the clearing that revealed these magnificent ruins, Pedro dropped his bag. As he bent over to pick it up, out of the corner of his eye, he caught a glimpse of someone very familiar.

"Señor Woody! I think we've got company," he whispered as he straightened up.

"Who?" Woodson asked. He looked over his shoulder just in time to see their old friend Roberto slip into the jungle and disappear. "Geez! There must have been another plane right after ours. See what happens when you stop for lunch!"

"But Blue was hungry, Woody," protested the young man.

Woodson just shook his head.

"She's always hungry. Never mind. C'mon, we'd better track down Lyons."

They ran toward the pyramid, dodging tourist's left and right, nearly knocking some down as they went along. When they reached the bottom of the ninety-one narrow stone steps that led to the temple at the top, they could see the nine sloped, step terraces that stand above the broad open square below. A member of the crew that removed the debris carelessly dropped by tourists as they climbed the steps of the pyramid was sweeping around the bottom of the stairway.

"Lyons, por favor?" Woodson called out to him.

The worker pointed directly at the gray stone face of the huge structure. Woodson knew exactly what he meant.

"He's inside, Pedro! He's probably up in the old temple chamber."

Pedro curled his fingers around Woodson's arm.

"We're going inside?" he gasped.

"Sure... It's no big deal, Pedro. It's a little cramped and a bit hot but nothing to be scared about."

"I'm not scared!" Pedro quickly replied, but Woodson could see the truth written on the young man's face.

As they reached the entrance to the old temple it was obvious that it had been closed off to the tourists for the day. Another worker, a smallish, dark man wearing a wrinkled khaki uniform, guarded the small opening that was constructed by archeologists many years before allowing them access to the inner pyramid. Upon recognizing Woodson, the guard immediately allowed them to enter.

The Maya did not tear down their temples; they built new ones over them using the older buildings as the base. Archeologists discovered the smaller temple within El Castillo during the pyramids restoration.

"Well, Pedro, it's been awhile since I've walked up these steps," he said as they proceeded up the dark and narrow stairway. The passageway was quite small, barely large enough for one person at a time. As they held on to the dark stonewalls, only inches from their shoulders, they could feel the weight of the damp, stale air as it filled their lungs. The only light to guide them was an occasional dimly lit electric bulb. "What do you think?"

Pedro looked nervously at his feet as they climbed the narrow staircase.

"It sure feels wet," he said, as the young man placed his hands firmly against the damp walls of the narrow passageway.

"Lyons—it's Woody. Are you up there?" he yelled, as they struggled up the stairs.

"Yes, yes. I've been waiting for you! Come up! Come up!" replied Professor Lyons impatiently, as if he had been disturbed from something extremely important.

Woodson stopped dead in his tracks. Pedro bumped into him and quickly lost his balance. Woodson reached back and grabbed his young friend. His strong grip on Pedro's shoulder was all that kept the young man from falling, backward, down the steps.

Woodson leaned toward Pedro and whispered, "How could he know we were coming? I only just decided to come here a few hours ago." Woodson paused. "Pedro," he began again," tell him nothing, and follow my lead. Got it?"

"Si Woody. But what do you think this is all about?"

"I'm not sure. But, I think that our friend Roberto and whoever he is working for are not the only ones looking for this." Woodson gave his backpack a quick tap and then continued up the dark and narrow stairway.

When they arrived at the top, it opened into a small chamber. It held two very ancient objects, the closest to them being a large stone Chac-mool, a statue used throughout the region during human sacrifice. From this the shaman priests would offer a still-beating human heart to the Gods. Further into the room, sitting close to the opposite wall, was a red painted stone Jaguar, its head was turned toward the entrance, its mouth open wide, with teeth bared to greet all that entered. Professor Lyons was kneeling over the odd, but mystical statue, inspecting one of the many jade stones that incrusted it.

Woodson spoke first upon seeing the professor.

"Still at it, I see," laughed Woodson. "You are obsessed with that thing. What now? Has it moved across the room under its own power?"

Lyons stood and turned around to greet his old friend. Robust and over sixty, Professor Lyons had silver hair, large hands and a broad smile. His tanned and wrinkled face spoke of the many years spent in this tropical climate. Lyons was Woodson's immediate supervisor, and had been very helpful in advancing his career.

"Woody, you son of a gun! It's great to see you," he said as he squeezed Woodson's hand with the strength of a much younger man. Then turning to Pedro, he added, "Pedro! How are you, my young amigo? You look more like your father every time I see you."

Professor Lyons, because of his long time friendship with the young man's father, and grandfather, had been responsible for Pedro's admission to the university at such a young age.

Woodson noticed that Pedro hesitated briefly before replying. "Gracias professor,"

"So Woody, what have you brought for me to see?" inquired Lyons curiously.

Woodson glanced at Pedro. After a brief silence, Woodson replied with a question.

"How did you know we were bringing something?"

Now Professor Lyons hesitated.

"Just a hunch, you've always liked to show me things that you uncover. But I am surprised that you left Tulum without contacting me first."

"Not to worry, Professor, I'm sure Julio's got it under control. And besides, the work was nearly done and no longer needed my direct attention."

"Well then, show me what you've got!"

Woodson hesitated.

"Maybe we should go back to the hotel. We're at the Mayaland, Blue is over there now."

"Blue! Blue is here too? I wasn't told.... Well, never mind, you head over there while I instruct my people how to finish up here. See you soon."

Pedro led the way back down the steps. When they had gotten about halfway to the outside entrance, he felt a firm grip on his shoulder. "Shh! don't make a sound," he heard Woodson whisper.

Pedro stood motionless and waited in silence. After several anxious moments he heard Professor Lyon's muffled voice.

"They're coming down now. Tell your men to get ready... No... Let them get to Mayaworld... The girl is there waiting for them... Good... I'll be there shortly!

"It seems that, our old friend, Lyons has forgotten how well voices carry down this stairwell," whispered Woodson. "I had a feeling he wasn't being straight with us. Look, when we get outside, act as if nothing is wrong. I'll stop at the Temple of Warriors before I head back to the hotel. You head directly to the main road. Just follow the tourists. Find Blue as fast as you can and wait for me in the car. I'll deal with Lyons later!"

Pedro nodded nervously as they emerged from the dark stairway. For the first time since the adventure began, he realized that he was afraid. Woodson quickly proceeded with the plan motioning to Pedro to make for the path to the exit. As they split up, Woodson noticed that he was being followed. As he quickly made for the building ahead, he looked over his shoulder and realized that the man following him was his old friend Roberto. Woodson quickly changed directions and started for the Plaza of a Thousand Columns, which is an arcaded walk containing row after row of square and rounded pillars. An excellent place to lose Roberto, he thought. As Woodson picked up his pace, so did his pursuer. Faster and faster he walked until he was at a dead run, but Roberto was still at his heels. When he reached the first row of columns Woodson began to dart from row to row in an attempt to lose Roberto in the maze of stone. Suddenly he tripped and fell rolling over onto his back. Roberto stood over Woodson pointing a pistol directly at his head.

"Please put that thing down before you hurt yourself, Roberto," said Woodson calmly, as he stood up and brushed the dirt off his shirt.

"The cylinder and the translations, Señor,"

demanded Roberto. "I think I will take them now. I do not want to shoot you."

"That works for me too." Woodson held up the bag, "I'll give you everything if you just tell me who you work for?"

"I work for a man who will pay quite a lot for what you carry in that bag, Señor—so hand it over now, or I will shoot!"

"Listen, I know for a fact that the authorities all over this site are looking for what's in this bag. So, I wouldn't be firing that pistol so fast," replied Woodson nonchalantly, still wiping the dust from his clothes.

Roberto looked nervously around the site. His hand was beginning to shake again. Woodson took a step toward him.

"If you're smart, you'll put the gun down so we can both get out of here!"

"No! Stand back! Hand that bag to me—now!"

Woodson shrugged his shoulders.

"Well, Roberto, you drive a hard bargain." Slowly he reached out to hand the bag to Roberto, and then just as the gunman was about to grab it, Woodson let it drop to the ground.

Roberto stepped back, the gun still pointing at Woodson.

"That won't work this time, Señor. Your young friend isn't here to hit me over the head."

Roberto had barely gotten the words out, when a

small, brown hand holding a large, gray rock, exploded out from behind the column he stood in front of. The rock hit Roberto solidly in the back of his head, leaving the gunman sprawled out onto the ground.

"Pedro?" asked Woodson in disbelief, "Is that you?"

Pedro peaked around the column grinning and chuckled, "Si."

"I thought I told you to find Blue?" scolded Woodson.

"But, Woody, I saved you—" Pedro attempted to reply, but was quickly cut off.

"Look Pedro, I could have handled this—" Woodson was interrupted by Roberto's groan as he started to come to. "Here, take this," he said as he handed Pedro the gun and knelt down next to the fallen man. "Who are you working for?" he demanded.

Roberto was still conscious. Rubbing his head, he looked up and saw Pedro's smiling face.

"You again!" he exclaimed.

"Who wants this cylinder?" Woodson persisted.

Roberto rubbed his head again and checked his hand for blood. He smiled briefly once he knew that his skull wasn't cracked.

"He said I should call him Aguilar." Roberto's tone became dark and serious. "I know nothing more about him, Señor—except that he really wants the papers you have. He has sworn to get them at any cost!"

"Another Aguilar?" cried Pedro, "This is getting really

weird, Woody. Can we please get out of here?"

Woodson gave Pedro a quick nod.

"Let's find Blue!" Then shoving his fist tightly up against Roberto's nose Woodson snarled, "If I were you I'd quit following us. You've been pretty lucky so far—next time my young friend here might just succeed in killing you— Pedro, grab my bag, we're out of here!"

CHAPTER SEVEN

On To Dzibilchaltún

Woodson and Pedro escaped down the path that led back to the entrance and on to the Mayaworld Hotel. As they reached the parking lot, a car bore down on them from between two parked tour buses. Woodson jumped back out of the way, barely pulling Pedro with him. As they fell to the ground, the car came to a screeching halt just next to where their bodies lay sprawled onto the pavement. The door flung open—it was Blue.

"What's wrong, Woody? Did you forget where we parked the car?" she laughed.

"You could have killed us!" he snapped.

"No way, I would never forgive myself if I hurt Pedro." she snickered. "Now hurry up and get your butts in the car!"

"How did you know that we were in trouble?" asked Woodson, quickly pulling Pedro to his feet.

"That's easy; you're always getting in trouble, so I decided to keep the motor running." Blue took a deep breath, "Then when I saw you and Pedro coming out of the jungle at a full run, I just figured my hunch was right, that you managed to screw things up again."

Woodson jumped into the front passenger seat and Pedro crawled into the back.

"For your information, I didn't screw up," began Woodson, "Lyons is after the journals as well!"

"Lyons knows?" she gasped.

"Not only that," cried Pedro, "we ran into that Roberto hombre again?"

"What? How did he get—?

"Because somebody wanted to stop for lunch!" exclaimed Woodson, pointing an accusing finger at her.

"But I was hungry," replied Blue.

"You're always hungry!" he sighed. "If you're going to drive, let's get out of here, now!"

Blue stepped on the gas only to quickly hit the brakes.

"Lyons!" she quickly exclaimed. "He's blocking the way!"

Professor Lyons stood directly in the center of the one lane road that led away from the ruins. Woodson turned to Blue.

"I'll handle this. Keep the motor running," he said while stepping out of the car.

"Why, Woody?" asked Lyons. "Why are you going to risk your career, even your life for what you found at Tulum?"

"Then you know what this is all about?" Woodson replied. "How did you know that I was coming here?"

Lyons eyed Woodson suspiciously.

"I really don't know what this is all about, but as far as how I knew you were coming here, that was easy: Julio called. What did you find Woody? What could be so important?"

"Look Professor, as you can see, I don't have much time to talk." Woodson pointed in the direction of the path leading to the ruins. "There are two armed guards heading our way. All I can tell you is that I think this is big, really big, and I need to see it through. Trust me on this Professor. Please!"

Pedro stuck his head out the window of the back seat.

"You have to trust Woody, Professor Lyons. He knows what he's doing!"

Lyons stared into Woodson's eyes, then glanced in Pedro's direction and smiled. Lyons stepped toward the car.

"Are you sure that your grandfather would approve of all this, Pedro?"

Pedro looked up at the professor.

"If Woody say's its okay—yes!"

Lyons stuck his hand into the car and patted the young man's chest affectionately. Turning back to Woodson said, "Push me down! Quickly!" he exclaimed

"What?" cried Woodson.

"C'mon Woody," said Lyons. "You don't have much time. Make it look good. Hurry!"

Woodson pushed Lyons down to the ground and rushed toward the car. From his back on the gravely drive, Lyons quickly gestured.

"Get out of here, Woody! Go!"

Woodson jumped back into the car. Blue hit the gas and the car's tires squealed against the hot asphalt and gravel road, kicking up a blinding cloud of smokey gray dust. By the time the guards reached Professor Lyons, the car had sped away down the road and out of sight.

"Are you all right, Professor?" asked the first guard to reach him, as he helped him to his feet.

"Yes, I think so," he replied softly. "The only thing hurt here is my pride. You know," Lyons continued, as he untied the neckerchief that he wore around his neck and wiped the sweat from his brow, "if I was a few years younger, I could have stopped him." Lyons brushed himself off and headed toward the hotel.

"Should we go after them, Professor Lyons?" asked one of the guards.

"Let them go!" exclaimed Lyons, looking back at the guards." Woodson knows this area better than most. We won't catch him. Not today anyway!"

Blue woke up to a room dimly lit by the small lamp on the desk. Woodson was slumped over the desk, deep in sleep. She glanced over at the other bed in the room, Pedro was asleep as well. It was three o'clock in the morning; she could tell that Woodson had been up most of the night translating the writings.

Rising, she quietly pulled the blanket from her bed and covered Woodson's shoulders. As she ran her fingers through his short brown hair, she thought of the odd circumstances that brought them together again. Blue looked down at sheets of yellow lined paper with Woody's scribbled translation still firmly set in his grasp. Slowly, and ever so carefully, she wrestled the papers free from his sleepy clutch. Kneeling down next to the desk, she held them up to the soft light and read the translations.

When we returned to Dzibilchaltún we were greeted with cheers and much celebration. The men were revered as mighty warriors that defeated the intruders upon Mayan soil. Even I became a hero to these people. It felt good to be home. I thought how funny it felt to call this place home. But by this time I felt as one with the Maya and Spain had become a very distant memory of another man. A man that I no longer knew and a memory that I had no longer any need of.

After a few days I visited Aguilar to tell him of what I had done. He was furious and cursed the day that I had been born. I explained that I had no choice. I begged and pleaded for him to understand what I had done and what I had become. Aguilar became a madman. He swore on his life that he would do everything in his power to avenge the deaths that I had caused. I had him restrained and with a heavy heart ordered Aguilar imprisoned until I had time to think.

That very night I had a vision in my sleep. I did not understand this vision for many years to come. It scared me for I had never experienced anything of the like before. But I will remember every detail of this vision until the day I die.

There was a Conquistador on a horse rearing up on its back legs. I could see that he was on a cliff. I did not recognize him. There were buildings there, but I did not recognize them. He rode the mighty steed down the hill into the center of the city where he stopped in front of a small stone altar. There I saw a smallish man dressed in the garb of a monk, throwing papers into a fire that sent its fiery fingers up to greet them. The fire gave light to the coming darkness and through the misty scene; I saw what looked like a *temple. I could also see the monk's face now; it was all contorted and appeared to be the face of the devil himself. But it was not the Devil whose face I saw. It was Aguilar's.*

I must have disturbed Zazhal ab. For when I awoke in a cold sweat, I found myself cradled in her arms. I did not fall back to sleep that night. The next morning, I went to Aguilar and released him.

Gonzalo Guerrero
As translated by R. Woodson

Blue had just finished the last word when she felt Woodson stir. Waking up with a start, he stared into her big blue eyes and smiled.

"You've read it?" he inquired sleepily.

"Yes, and It's getting really weird. Guerrero's nightmare sounded horrible!"

Woodson rubbed the sleep from his eyes.

"I know. I still don't know where all of this is going to take us."

Blue placed her hand on his and closed her eyes for a moment.

"Do you think Lyons is right? Will you lose everything?" she asked.

"No way, Blue! I'll figure this out. Don't worry." he

said, changing his tone to upbeat.

"But what if Lyons is right?"

"I guess I'll cross that bridge when I come to it. Besides, even if I do lose my job, there are plenty of other things I can do," he said with a wink.

"Like what, Woody?"

"I can play the guitar. I'll join a band," he said playfully.

"You only know three chords."

"Okay... I'm a funny guy. Maybe I'll go to Hollywood and write sit-com scripts for a living."

"You're not that funny. Now get serious for a minute would you?"

"Okay... How about this? I've always wanted to be a personal trainer. I'm in pretty good shape. I could—"

"That's it," grouched Blue. "I'm going back to sleep and I suggest you do the same."

"Look Blue," began Woodson, "I don't know if you can understand it, but this whole thing has gotten under my skin. I feel some kind of connection with this Guerrero character. I can't explain it, but I need to see this through."

"Until what?"

"Until it ends, I guess. I'm not sure where this will take me... us," he said, glancing over at the snoring Pedro. "But I think our young friend here will be able to help."

"Pedro? He's just a boy. What in the world could he

possibly have to do with all this?"

Woodson took his notes from her and stared down at the messy yellow sheets.

"I'm not sure. I just have this feeling that he somehow fits into all of this, that's all."

"I don't understand any of this, Woody; not yet anyhow. But, if you feel so strongly about it, I will try to help any way I can." Blue pointed toward the bed. "Now, let's get some sleep, I'm sure we could all use it."

"Wait. Not just yet, Blue. I need to tell you something. Something I have never told another living soul."

Blue could tell he was dead serious.

"What is it?" she inquired softly.

Woodson paused to collect his thoughts before answering.

"When I was in my teens, not much older than Pedro, I was home sick on New Years Eve. All my friends were at a big party, and I was feeling pretty bummed out and sorry for myself. Not feeling too well, I went to sleep early, long before midnight. Then it happened!"

"What happened?"

"I had the most incredible dream… no, the word nightmare would describe it better. I saw a man, a white man, in a dugout canoe. I sensed that he was with an Indian woman though I don't remember seeing her. But she was there, I'm sure of it. Then the scene changed to what looked like a Spanish Conquistador dressed in full battle armor riding down a hill on horseback." He paused and took a deep breath before continuing. "Quickly the scene changed back to the people in the canoe and—the man was on fire."

"How awful. How did he catch on fire?"

"I can't say. But then the most remarkable thing happened. I could actually feel my skin burning. It was terrible. It felt so real... like I was there. I must have cried out because the next thing I remembered was my dad trying to wake me up. The dream haunted me for some time after that night, but I was eventually able to put it out of my mind. I think I forgot about it altogether until..."

"What? Until what, Woody?"

"The very first time I visited the ruins at Tulum. As I walked around the ruins, I had a sense that I had been there before. Then, without thought or warning, the memories of this nightmare flooded back into my consciousness. The haunting nightmare came back to me right there in the middle of the day. The feelings were so strong, I felt as if I was going to pass out. It felt as if I were possessed or something."

"This is pretty heavy stuff. I think you should get some professional help. I know a really good therapist—"

"No jokes, Blue. This is serious." He held up a page of Guerrero's journal to the light. "What ever is going on in these pages—it's part of me. I can feel it and I need to find out why!"

"We need to find out why!" she said softly. "I told you—I would help you in any way I could—please believe that."

Nodding, he dropped the sheets of paper back on the desk, looked up and smiled.

Blue smiled back, grabbed the blanket and went back to her bed. Woodson turned out the light and stepped to the other bed. Pedro was in the middle of the bed snoring away like a buzz- saw. Gently, he pushed Pedro over to the other side being careful not to wake him.

Except for Pedro's snoring, the room was quiet. Woodson laid there for a while, in silence, thinking about all that he and Blue had discussed. Then whispering, so he wouldn't wake Pedro, Woodson called out to her.

"Blue?"

"What?" she whispered back impatiently. "I'm trying to get some sleep!"

"I'm really glad you're here."

For a few moments the room fell silent again, except of course for Pedro's snoring. When there was no response, Woodson decided to roll over and try to get some sleep, when he heard her reply, "Me too, Woody. Me too," she said softly.

It was barely after dawn as they made their way through the ruined city of Dzibilchaltún. The sun was breaking through the clouds and the patchy fog that partially hid this ruined city was lifting to expose this important archeological site that spread out over nearly seven square miles. Most of the buildings had been reduced to rubble after the jungle reclaimed the city some time after the Spanish Conquest, but many still remained. As they walked along, Blue shot frequent glances over her shoulder, as if waiting for something to happen.

Woodson reached out grabbed her shoulder stopping her dead in her tracks.

"Stop that," he said. "You're making me nervous!"

"Could you explain how we got in here without anybody questioning why we're here at the break of day?" she asked.

"Easy. I had Pedro call his uncle, Armando, who just happens to be the head of security here. Any other questions?"

"Yeah! Why didn't the cops chase us, or figure out that we were going to be here... just like at Chicken Pizza?"

"Here," he replied, "take a look at what Lyons stuffed into Pedro's pocket in the parking lot at Chichén Itzá."

"When—?"

"When he came over to the car, he stuffed it into

Pedro's pocket. Pedro didn't even know it. He found the note this morning."

Blue took the note.

Woody,

I'm not sure exactly what is going on, but I do trust your judgment. I hope the words that I say to you today will not come to pass. I will do everything I can to stall the police. But I must know what is going on. I will be expecting your call. I will be staying at the Mayaland for two more days. I will be in my room both days during the lunch hour. Call me. I want to help.

Lyons.

"Now, that's interesting," she said. "Is he with us or against us? And what are we doing here?"

He pointed toward an unusual square building. The building sat atop a small platform with what appeared to be a dozen steps leading to it. The small stone temple had a large doorway on each of the four cardinal points of the compass with windows on each side of the doorways that faced east and west.

"What is that Woody?" asked Pedro as they approached the building.

"The Temple of the Seven Dolls, Pedro," he replied.

"I thought so. We studied this site last semester. This is my first time here," said Pedro excitedly. "Are we going in?"

"We sure are!" Woodson turned to Pedro and spoke to him softly. Blue couldn't make out what he was saying, but she was sure that he was giving Pedro directions.

"Si Woody, I'll check with Armando," responded Pedro to whatever Woodson had requested.

"See if he has a Polaroid or any kind of camera in the office. Pictures would be much better than tracings if we need to copy anything in there," added Woodson.

Woodson watched Pedro run off and then turned to Blue.

"After you," he said, as he gestured for her to ascend the broken, ancient steps. The steps were like most in ancient Mayan ruins, narrow and high with large cracks that made for less than sure footing. Blue navigated the steps quickly. Woodson was right behind her.

"What was that all about?" asked Blue once inside the temple.

"I just wanted Armando to keep the temple off limits until we were finished."

"Woody, did you ever see the dolls that they found here?"

"No, just pictures. The seven clay dolls that were found here are in a museum somewhere."

"What do you expect to find here anyway?"

"Not sure, but I hope to find another message from the past."

"But haven't you been here before? Don't you think

you would have seen something that was out of the ordinary?"

"My perspective would have been different. I think I know what I am looking for now."

The two entered the temple. The chill of the damp morning air made the ruins feel cold and empty. The room smelled of untold years of being exposed to the elements. As they moved about they disturbed a large iguana from its slumber. Blue screamed as it brushed against her leg while it scurried quickly for the doorway. When Woodson looked up in response to the noise, his eyes caught something he had never seen before. Slowly, he walked over to the window that lay to the left of the west doorway. Bending over he rubbed the stone that lay just below the window. He rubbed away the dirt and mud that had collected over the centuries, a small drawing appeared. It was very small and painted on, not the usual carved image.

"Look! There is something here. I knew it!" he said using his sleeve to wipe away the dirt. "Blue, what do you see?"

Just at that moment Pedro stepped into the temple carrying a small disposable camera.

Blue carefully leaned over to see what her companion had uncovered.

"Look at that. Two white men, both wearing beards. One is dressed like Maya, the other... a Conquistador."

"That's it!" he exclaimed. "Look at this figure—the

Conquistador—his back is turned to the other."

Pedro dropped to his knees to get a better look.

"Yeah, like he was walking away. But to where?" he asked.

Woodson rubbed away more dirt being careful not to disturb any of the drawing. Suddenly he stopped rubbing and stepped back.

"There it is, Pedro. Go ahead, take a look."

As the young man took a closer look, he gasped in disbelief. There before him was a shape he knew well, the shape of the island where he lived with his grandfather.

"Woody—that's Cozumel!" he gasped. "This drawing depicts the parting of Guerrero and Aguilar!"

"Do you really think that Guerrero made this drawing?" asked Blue.

Pedro replied before Woodson could utter a single a word.

"Who else," he said excitedly while the flash of the disposable camera fired rapidly, recording everything they had just found in the small temple.

Woodson smiled at his young apprentice.

"I think it's time to go see Angel!"

CHAPTER EIGHT

Aguilar Leaves for Cozumel

It has been almost two years since I last saw Aguilar. When I released him, neither of us spoke. As he walked into the morning sun, I do not remember if he even looked back. I miss him; I had heard stories of Aguilar. Whether they were true, I did not know. I did hear, from a trader, that he had met another, like me, not so very long ago, maybe a year. He told me of this man that had fallen into the hands of people, in a small city not far from here. Upon further questioning, the trader could not remember any more than the cacique was holding my old friend as a slave. At least, I knew there was a good chance that Aguilar still lived. Over the next few days, I gave much thought to attempting a rescue. Would Aguilar even come with me if I did? I would need to think more.

Some days had passed; I was sitting

before my fire. It was dusk and I was resting from the day with my evening meal, when a figure stepped out of the shadows and stood over me. It was Aguilar! He just stood there for a long time. Not a word was spoken by either of us. Finally he sat beside me. He spoke of his experiences since we saw each other last. He then told me something that I had expected for some time.

The Spanish had returned. They were in Cuzamil and it was Cortez himself who sent a messenger for us. He begged for me to go with him. I told him it was too late for me. I loved my family. I loved these people. I had no reason to go back. He showed me Cortez' message but I refused to read it. My wife became very angry and demanded that Aguilar leave and never dare to return to this city again.

Aguilar handed me some green beads, which were sent by Cortez, to free me from my captors. I smiled and hugged my old friend and watched him walk away until he was out of sight. I hoped that he made Cuzamil in safety and good health.

I then went to my wife's father, the High Priest and leader of the city, and explained the troubling circumstances. The Spanish were here and the Conquest had begun. The high priest told of a place of hiding where my family and I would be safe. I had thought The Lost City was only a legend. It now seemed that it really did exist. Our escape was planned and we were to leave by the next moon.

The day before we were to leave, the High Priest came to me and presented me with what looked to be a codex wrapped in deerskin. He told me these were sacred writings of the Maya and they should be kept from the invaders. He would entrust their safekeeping to me. I had studied such codex to learn of the Mayan ways and language. Many days Zazhal ab would help me learn the meaning of the writings and glyphs painted on the bark of fig trees. I knew of their importance to the Maya. He spoke of a vision; a vision of a man dressed in robes burning all the sacred writings of his people. It was the same vision as I had experienced but now I understood. I expressed to Kin, the High Priest my deep affection and respect for him and my love for his daughter. I assured him that I would do everything *in my power to protect his daughter, his grandsons and the codex.*

The next morning my family and I set out for an unknown place.

Gonzalo Guerrero
As translated by R Woodson

"Woody, are you there?" asked Blue, as she kicked the large wooden door to the room. "Open up Woody. My hands are full and I can't reach my key!"

After a few seconds the door opened wide. Blue was greeted with Woodson's beaming smile.

"What are you so happy about?" she asked.

"Blue! You are not going to believe what Pedro and I... What is all that stuff you're holding?"

"Food, you big dope! A girl's got to eat doesn't she?" Woodson and Pedro watched as Blue waltzed into the room and dump her precious cargo on the bed. Woodson never tired of looking at Blue. He thought of how stupid he was to let her slip away. "So, what am I not going to believe now?" she inquired sarcastically.

"Oh yeah," said Woodson as he snapped out of it. "I think I know what we're looking for now."

"Hello! I thought we decided that it was some lost city," said Blue, while biting into a large tortilla.

"No, Blue! Pedro thinks we're looking for another codex." Blue stood there in silence, her mouth hanging wide open.

"Please, close your mouth?" requested Pedro, "that's pretty gross!"

"Sorry Pedro." she turned to Woodson. "Woody, that's impossible. Where can it be? How could it be that we haven't heard of this before?"

"Look, I'm not sure, but I think that there might just be a fifth codex out there. That would explain why everyone is chasing us."

"What?"

"Here. You sit down and eat while I explain," said Woodson, as he sat her down on the edge of the bed. "Now, listen carefully. If there were a real lost city, which seems most unlikely, what would be the big deal? Someone would eventually find it. People like us would study and restore it, the tourists would visit it, and that would be the end of it, right?"

Blue stood up, as if to ask a question, but Woodson pressed a hand on her shoulder to sit her back down.

"I'm not finished yet. Sit tight." Woodson collected his thoughts. "Now, if someone were to find another codex—one that could possibly be the key to solving the mystery of the missing Mayan writings and culture—that would be worth something."

Blue just sat and stared at him in disbelief, slowly chewing her tortilla and shaking her head.

"Okay, Blue. Now try and keep up. As we speak, we have only translated and interpreted… maybe sixty percent of the Mayan language. What if this holds the key to the rest of the language? There are only four other codice, one in Dresden, one in Paris, one in Madrid and the Grolier, though quite a bit of the Grolier Codex had been destroyed, giving us very little information. These are the only original writings of the ancient Maya. That would make a fifth codex priceless."

"Woody I know about the four codice. Do you really think that everyone is after us because they think what we are chasing is valuable? Valuable enough for them to shoot at us?"

"Why else? How could a lost city bring riches to anyone? But if there was a Fifth Codex, that would be something." Woodson began to pace again, nearly bumping into walls and furniture in the cramped hotel room. Suddenly he stopped, looked up and slapped himself sharply in the forehead.

"Oh, Woody, I bet that smarts," teased Pedro.

"What's wrong?" asked Blue, trying not to laugh.

"Since he's still in school Pedro probably knows more about this subject than either of us!" Woodson turned to his assistant. "Popol Vuh! What if we are talking about the Popol Vuh? What if it was the Mayan book of the dawn of life? It's got to be somewhere doesn't it?"

"That's impossible, Woody!" replied Pedro.

Woodson began pacing back and forth again.

"Why?"

"First of all, the actual book of Popol Vuh was probably destroyed by the friars during the Conquest. Secondly, we are talking about the wrong region, the Popol Vuh was written in the highlands of Guatemala. The chances are slim to none that it would fall into the hands of a Spaniard in the lowlands of the Yucatan."

"Wow kid, you really know your stuff!" Woodson walked over and picked up a package of food. Blue slapped his hand and smiled. "Get your own. These are mine."

Woodson dropped the package and rubbed his hand vigorously.

"Pedro's right, it can't be the Pool Vuh!" insisted Blue

"The Popol Vuh is one of the most sacred writings in the history of the Maya," began Woodson, "It relates to the beginning of their history. Pedro, if it wasn't for the friars forcing the Maya to learn the Roman alphabet and translating the stories and legends into Spanish, this information could have been lost forever. Why not the Yucatan? Why not Guerrero? How do we know this high priest wasn't the keeper of this wonderful document?"

"Okay, Woody, even if you're right, then what?" asked Pedro.

Woodson sat down at the desk and ran his hands slowly through his hair.

"I'm not quite sure yet. At this point all we can do is

continue translating this thing," he said pointing toward the papers that were neatly laid out on the desk. "You both better get some rest. We leave bright and early tomorrow for Playa del Carmen."

"And then, Cozumel! You know Woody this is starting to get exciting!" said Blue while chewing a mouthful of tortilla chips.

"Starting? Oh brother! C'mon Pedro, let's get some sleep and leave Blue to her snacks!"

"Is she always hungry?" asked Pedro.

"A bottomless pit, my young friend!"

Roberto stood on the pier in Playa del Carmen. It was noon, the time that he had been instructed to be there. The day was beautiful. Not a cloud in the sky. A soft breeze was blowing in off the blue-green Caribbean. He could hear the children playing soccer on the beach. He smelled the native dishes being prepared on open grills in the square.

Roberto knew that he probably should not have come, having failed Aguilar again, but the handsome pay he would receive for his efforts was difficult to resist. From the pier he watched the blue and white ferry gliding smoothly into the dock from Cozumel. Lost in thought, Roberto hadn't noticed that he had been bumped by a passerby. Might I have been mistaken in the time I was to meet Aguilar, he thought. Roberto glanced up and down the crowded pier for any sign of

Aguilar. It wasn't long before he heard a soft, husky voice directly behind him.

"Roberto! Do not turn around!" Roberto didn't move. "Bueno. You will find a ticket in your left hip pocket. Get on the ferry and sit as far to the rear as you can. I will find you. When I do, act as if we are strangers. Comprende." Roberto nodded quickly but still looked straight ahead. "Now go!"

Roberto reached deeply into his pocket, to his surprise the ticket was there. A cold shudder ran down his back at the thought of Aguilar placing the ticket in his pocket without him knowing it. Trying not to think anymore, he made for the pier and boarded the ferry. The boat was wide with rows of comfortable looking seats. The sides were open to give the passengers a spectacular view of the sea and San Miguel as it approached the Island of Cozumel. Quickly he made for the rear of the passenger area, sitting in the last row one seat in from the aisle. As he settled into the seat, a round looking little man wearing a white hat and jacket approached. It must be Aguilar, he thought, he had yet to see the man in the light of day.

"Excuse me, Señor," said the man in white. "Is this seat taken?"

Roberto gestured that it was not. The little man in the white hat took the seat.

"Now, you will listen again. Eh, Roberto? You will smile and nod as I speak. I will tell you exactly what I want you to do when we get to San Miguel. Now, smile and nod... Very good Roberto! When we get to port I want you to rent a car.

"There is a credit card and ID already in your other pocket; I suggest you get to know what your new name is before you use it. That's it... Smile and nod... After you do this, I want you to drive to the southern end of the island. There, you will check into the resort under the name on your credit card. There is an Italian restaurant upstairs. I want you to keep an eye on the manager. His name is Angel; small man with a round face and squinty eyes. You will know him when you see him. I do not want you to concern yourself with your past failures. I will still pay you handsomely for your services." Aguilar stood and without another word disappeared into a group of people crowded at the front of the boat. Roberto looked out over the rolling waters and wondered, and worried, where this adventure would finally lead him.

"Why are we stopping?" asked Blue, as Pedro pulled off the road into the only gas station in Valladolid, a colonial town that rests in the center of the Yucatan Peninsula.

"It's the noon hour Blue. Time to call Lyons, if I can reach the phone. Look at all the tour buses stopped here. Last stop before Chichén Itzá, I guess. Well, here goes." Woodson didn't take one step before hearing

Pedro's voice.

"Woody."

He turned back to the car.

"Can we trust him?" asked Pedro. "Do you think we should talk to my grandfather before you talk to Lyons?"

"No, I'm not sure if we should trust him, Pedro. I'm just going to see if he wants to set something up. We will definitely talk to Angel before meeting with him."

Woodson left the car and carefully walked toward to the station, avoiding a group of tourists descending on the poor attendant for bottled water. Finally reaching the phone, he removed his hat and wiped the hot afternoon sweat from his brow. He inserted his phone card and dialed the Mayaworld Hotel.

"Yes, Professor Lyon's room, por favor... Gracias, Señor."

As Woodson waited to be connected, he had the unmistakable feeling that he was being watched. Nonchalantly, Woodson scanned the area through the throngs of tourists. He couldn't say from where, but someone was watching.

"Yes, Lyons, it's Woody," he said, once the connection was made. "Yes we're okay for now... I can't say exactly what we are looking for, but I think I am getting close to figuring it out... Someone else is extremely interested in what we are looking for as well... Never mind that, if you really want to help, meet us in Cozumel—we should be in Playa del Carmen in a few hours. We'll hop the first ferry out to San Miguel. If you're interested in helping, meet me tomorrow night at 6:00 pm at La Mission Restaurant... I will tell you everything I know then... Good... I will see you tomorrow!"

Woodson hung up the phone and walked slowly toward the car. The tour buses were pulling out on to the highway, kicking up a smoke and dust clouding the air. As the air began to clear, he noticed that a large black car had pulled in front of the station. A tall, dark man dressed in white and wearing dark glasses, climbed through the driver door of the limo and quickly pulled away. Woodson ran to his car and stuck his head through the open passenger window.

"Did either of you notice that black car?" he asked.

"Si, Woody," said Pedro, "It came out from behind the station. It must have been parked there."

"Geez! Now who's following us?" He jumped into the passenger seat. "Step on it Pedro... let's get a better look at that guy!"

"You got it Boss!" he exclaimed. Pedro stepped on the gas and the car peeled away from the station throwing up a great cloud of white dust behind it.

"Are you two crazy?" cried Blue. "You're going to get us killed Woody!"

Woodson ignored Blue's protests.

"Get as close as you can Pedro," he shouted, "I want to see his face!"

Pedro stepped on the gas again. The car lunged forward throwing Blue, who had been leaning toward the front seat, back hard against her seat.

"Hey! Are you guys crazy?" she screamed as her head bounced off the back seat as Pedro floored it again.

The engine whined as Pedro pushed the pedal all the way to the floor. They were quickly gaining on the limo. The other driver quickly realized that they were being followed and answered by accelerating to open up some distance between the two vehicles.

Pedro downshifted but never let up on the gas as they sped around a tight bend in the road, bringing them closer to the other car. The larger limo needed to slow down to better navigate the curve.

"Where did you learn to drive like that?" hollered Woodson with a smile.

"Angel!" exclaimed Pedro, as he shifted the car back into fourth gear.

"Gun it again and pull up next to him!" cried Woodson.

"I'm on it Woody!" replied Pedro. His voice shook with excitement.

Pedro downshifted again as they fast approached the next turn in the road. The black limo was beginning to spit white clouds of dusty smoke from its rear tires as it slid into the turn just ahead of them.

"Now!" screamed Woodson.

Pedro smashed the gas pedal into the floor again. Sweat was pouring from the young man's forehead, but he did not dare to take a hand off the wheel to wipe it away. The car lunged forward throwing Blue back into the seat again.

"Stop!" she screamed. Pedro steered the car into the opposite lane and downshifted again. There was a loud thud from the backseat. "Ouch!"

"What was that?" hollered Pedro, as he veered the car even closer to the limo.

"Nothing—just Blue hitting the side of the car." Woodson pointed toward the road ahead. "Just drive!"

The engines of both cars roared loudly as Pedro pulled the car even with the limo.

"There's a passenger too!" Woodson exclaimed loudly. "Pull up closer!" Pedro steered the car to the right until Woodson's passenger door was only a few feet from the limo's driver door. "I can see their faces, Pedro. Try and hold it—" Woodson paused, "UH OH... HE'S GOT A GUN—DUCK!"

There was an explosion and the car's windshield shattered on the passenger's side. Pedro quickly turned the wheel toward the limo and side swiped it before hitting the brakes. The limo lurched and bounced before it ran off the bumpy pavement onto the even bumpier gravel shoulder in a cloud of smoky dust before speeding away.

Pedro steered the car off to the side of the road

and turned off the engine.

"Is everybody okay?" asked Woodson.

"What was that all about?" cried Blue, as she picked herself up from the car floor.

Pedro finally got to wipe the sweat from his brow as he tilted his head back and looked up at the roof of the car.

"Where did you learn to do that, Pedro?" asked Woodson, then holding up his hand said, "Never mind—Angel, right? That was a nice piece of driving, Kid."

Pedro nodded and restarted the car.

"What now Woody?"

"Head for Playa del Carmen, but keep a sharp eye out for that limo."

Blue pulled herself up in between the two front seats.

"Could somebody please tell me what that proved?" she asked irritably.

"I got a good look at those two," said Woodson, as he started to calm down. "They're the security guy's from Chichén Itzá. This is getting weirder by the minute. What are they doing in a big black limo—and following us?"

"Maybe they're not security guards at all!" said Pedro as he slowly pulled the car back onto the road.

Woodson didn't reply.

CHAPTER NINE

Angel Saves The Day

"Angel! You son of a gun! How the are you, amigo?" yelled Woodson across the quiet, empty dining room. Angel was busily preparing the restaurant for the first dinner seating. Having managed the restaurant for many years Angel was a great favorite of the guests. Below average height and in his mid sixties, Angel still had plenty of jet-black hair that framed his round face with a pleasant and toothy smile. A practicing shaman, or holy man, Angel had a knowledge and wisdom of all things Maya - ancient and modern.

Angel was one of the first people Woodson had befriended when he first came to the Yucatan on vacation, years ago. Woodson had been a professor at the time, teaching archeology at the university. He and Angel hit it off immediately, and became good friends from the very start. Woodson never did quite understand why he felt so close, so quickly, to the old shaman—whatever it was, he accepted it.

It was Angel that convinced him to devote more time to studying Mayan culture. "Come back some day to help restore the ancient sites," Angel told him. "I believe it is your destiny." It was the best advice that Woodson had ever received. Now there was nowhere on earth that he loved more that the Yucatan, and very few people he felt closer to then Pedro and Angel. They were his Maya family.

"Woody! Come here to your old friend," cried Angel with delight.

Woodson had made it only about halfway across the restaurant when he saw Angel's expression suddenly change. His old friend had spotted Blue, who was standing in the doorway just behind Woodson.

"Blue? This is a great day for Angel."

He rushed past Woodson's open arms, right into Blue's waiting arms. Angel gave her a big hug and a kiss. Woodson placed his hands on his hips, and shook his head.

"What am I, chopped liver?" he griped.

"Oh, it is so good to see you both again," gushed Angel. He turned to Woodson. "Are you here on vacation?"

"Nope, I wish we were," said Woodson. "Actually we're here to see you. We need your help old friend."

"Anything for my good friends," smiled Angel, "You know that."

"We might have to take you up on that," said Blue, as Angel pinched both of her cheeks. "Whoa! Take it easy partner those things are attached."

"Sorry Blue, I am just so glad to see you! Where is

my grandson? Is he with you?"

"Pedro is stowing our gear," said Woodson. "He'll be along directly."

"So tell me, my friends, what brings you to Angel?"

Woodson sat down at a table and motioned for Angel to join him. Blue stood behind Angel's chair and placed her hands affectionately on the older man's shoulders. The shaman sat quietly and listened politely as his friends told all of what had occurred over the last few days.

Once they had finished, Angel said nothing. He thought for a moment, then, placing one of his hands on Blue's asked, "What can I do to help?"

"Look, I don't want to keep you from your work," said Woodson. "But we really need you to go with us to San Gervasio tomorrow morning. Can you swing it?"

"San Gervasio? Why?" asked Angel.

"Blue thinks that little Mayan city has some answers. Plus nobody on this island knows those ruins like you do," replied Woodson.

"Si, I was one of the first volunteers to help clear the site back in 1970. But, how can that help you?"

"You let me worry about that. We're going to check into our rooms. Pedro will probably stop up to see you later—" Woodson hesitated as he spied Pedro in the doorway. "—Wait, here he is now!"

Angel's eyes could have lit a darkened room when he saw his grandson walk through the door.

"Pedro!" he exclaimed jumping quickly to his feet. "How is my favorite grandson?"

"I'm your only grandson," Pedro replied sarcastically, but with a warm smile.

"Come give your grandfather a hug!" Angel demanded playfully.

"We've brought Angel up to date on everything, Pedro," began Woodson, "Blue and I will let you two catch up on things while we go wash up."

Woodson turned and started for the door. Then, just as he put his hand on the knob, he turned back to Angel.

"What are the chances for three at the eight thirty seating tonight, Angel?" he asked, as if he didn't already know the answer.

"It's very busy and I'm all booked up but—" Angel shook his head and smiled. "I'll see what I can do." Then he pointed at old friend. "He never changes does he Blue?"

"Unfortunately, no," she chuckled.

Angel grabbed Pedro behind the neck.

"You look thin, Pedro," he said with a broad grin. "Come into the kitchen and I'll make you something to eat."

"I'm fine Grandfather," Pedro protested.

"Don't argue with Angel," said Woodson, who was still in the doorway.

Angel waved to Woodson and Blue and happily

dragged his reluctant grandson to the kitchen.

The journey was a difficult time for my family. My three sons were still very young. My wife never let on to how she felt. I think, though she never told me, that she was ill for most of the journey. Whenever necessary we carried the children, forcing us to rest often. Our guides and protectors were very helpful, and the people in the villages where we stopped showed us great hospitality.

We made our way through much dense and dry brush, staying on small paths that went on forever. Finally one morning, after spending the night camped near a small cenote, our path led us to a sacbé, a road made from stones as are in the cities. I was amazed that we had found such a road in the jungle, so far from any city. When I inquired as to why the Maya had built these roads; our guide explained that after many life cycles in the past (the Maya consider a life cycle complete after fifty-two years) this road was built to connect the great cities of the north to the city by the sea. He further explained that this enabled the traders access to sea travel, the coastal villages and to allow the Maya in this region to travel north to Chichén Itzá and the Sacred Cenote.

As the coast grew nearer, there were more villages and small farms. Most nights we had a decent place to rest and enough food and water. The villagers were always willing to share and all they wanted in return was news of the great cities to the north. With the comfort of these villages to rest at, my wife grew stronger. My sons adapted well to this difficult time. Zazhal ab would fill the time we rested by teaching our boys about the sacred writings that we carried with us. With only the night fires for light she would read to our sons until they fell asleep. To my surprise, the words she read were not of the same fashion as the texts that I had read during my studies. This codex had more of a religious tone and seemed most strange and frightening. These words scared her so that she would no longer read them to our children. We did not speak of it again for the rest of our journey.

The road led us to a large city. The

city was in a state of ruin; the population was so sparse it seemed deserted. This place must have been glorious at one time. It had the tallest steepest pyramid I had seen since coming to this world. In addition, the most peculiar thing about the area was the presence of lakes. Nowhere in my travels had I seen one lake, much less a group of lakes. Our guides explained that this was once a great city called Coba. I could feel this as I stood at the base of the great pyramid they called Nohoch Mull, as it towered over the rest of the city. I was told that it was the people from this city that built the sacred road we traveled. Remarkably they constructed this road to maintain control over their trade and political interests in the north near Chichén Itzá. These people never cease to amaze me with their accomplishments. We rested for a few days at this city and then set out for, as our guides called it, Tulum, the City of Walls.

Gonzalo Guerrero

As translated by R. Woodson

The tiny Jeep pitched and bounced as it traveled from pothole to pothole on the narrow road that led to the ruins at the hacienda, San Gervasio. Hidden by the dense brush and thickly treed jungle, this small but important site in Mayan culture lay several miles north of the main road that connects the city of San Miguel and the windward, nearly deserted side of the island of Cozumel.

Pedro was again at the wheel with Woodson in the front passenger seat. Angel and Blue attempted to sit in the backseat, but because of the deep potholes, spent much of the ride, suspended in air, inches above the seat. The sun had only just risen, but the heat of the jungle greeted them harshly as they drove deeper into the thick brush.

"Woody!" Angel yelled trying to be heard over the noise of the engine and the bumpy road. "What do you expect to find here this morning?"

"If I'm right, Angel, Guerrero will have left us another message," replied Woodson.

"But, I have worked this site for years," began Angel, "I have never seen anything like what you found at the Temple of the Seven Dolls."

Pedro looked in the rearview mirror and started to chuckle. Angel and Blue looked like rag-dolls as they bounced up and down in the back seat.

"Woody had been in that temple many times before, Angel" said Pedro loudly, as he tried to focus on his bouncing grandfather in the rearview mirror. "But he never saw what was on that wall. Maybe it will be the same at this place!"

"Hey Pedro, you missed a pothole back there," yelled Blue sarcastically as she bounced off of her seat and nearly landed in Angel's lap.

Pedro was still laughing as the road finally ended in a small, white, gravel parking lot. Pedro parked the Jeep under the shade of a scrawny, white and black spotted tree. As they approached the main gate to the ruins, a small, dark, neatly dressed older gentleman stepped out of the shadows to stop them.

"The park is closed," he snapped. Then, upon spotting Angel, threw up his hands with delight. "Angel, my friend, it is so good to see you. Why are you here so early?"

Angel took the man by his arm and spoke softly in his ear.

"The Señor Woodson!" The man peeked shyly around Angel to get a better look. "Why of course my friend," he said. As the two friends shook hands, it was apparent that Angel had placed something into the old man's hand. The man smiled revealing two gold teeth and agreed to let them into the park.

"Is this your grandson, Pedro?" asked the man, as Pedro attempted to pass.

"Of course, this is little Pedro," said Angel proudly.

"He's not so little anymore, Angel," replied the man

as he shook the young man's hand.

Pedro blushed but remained polite as Angel introduced him and the others to his old friend. Once inside the ruins Angel decided to take the lead.

"Where to first, Woody?"

Woodson stopped in his tracks and folded his arms across his chest.

"You know Angel, when I'm here, I always feel... I don't know... at home would be the best way to put it. I'm not sure why. Let's walk the sacbé to the Big House, I think that's where we should start." Then turning to his young apprentice said, "What do you think, Pedro, Big House?"

"That makes the most sense," Pedro replied to his mentor. "Except for the small doorways on either side, the building is nearly enclosed and well protected from the elements. If Guerrero has left us a message, it will be at the Big House!"

Woodson gave Angel a wink. "Excellent, Pedro, that's exactly what I thought."

Carefully, they made their way down the thousand-year-old limestone road. The Maya were master road builders. Hundreds of miles of these limestone roads have been found throughout the Yucatan Peninsula. The Maya called them, sacbé, or sacred road. These roads connected the great cities for purposes of trade and alliances. When the sacbé were originally built, the white limestone would gleam brightly in the sun. Now most of the ancient roads have been swallowed up by the region's dense brush jungle, or have disappeared completely.

After so many years, the jungle had nearly destroyed this road as it reclaimed the small city. Navigating the rocks was difficult, but the small group answered the challenge. Soon they were standing at the arch that marked the road leading to the building called, Big House Structure.

"Pedro," said Angel, "Please lead the way!"

After a while, Angel turned and gave Woodson a puzzled look.

"What is it Woody? You seem to have something on your mind." he asked.

"Let's fall back a little so Pedro and Blue won't hear. I need to ask you about somebody named Aguilar."

Angel stopped suddenly.

"Keep walking, my friend," said Woodson. Angel took a couple of quick steps, to catch up to Woodson. "Looks like you might know him."

"He is an evil man Woody. You must stay away from him!"

"It seems that he can't stay away from us."

"How do you mean?"

"He's the guy who has a man trailing us. Like I told you yesterday, he has tried to steal my translations of Guerrero's writings twice. If it weren't for Pedro, he'd have them. Aguilar obviously knows about these writings and seems to have the same goal as we do."

"Why did you not tell me about him before?" asked Angel.

"I wanted to ask you in private. I'm thinking this guy Aguilar is a pretty bad dude." Woodson paused for a moment. "I figured that you'd know about him, and that my suspicions about him were right."

Angel stopped again. Looking around, he called out to Pedro and Blue, who had been in an animated discussion as to where they should go to lunch. Angel held up his index finger to his lips, signaling for quiet.

"Someone is watching us, Amigo! I can tell," he hissed.

"Maybe it's your friend, the guard," said Pedro.

"No, I do not think so. Let us continue down this road. When we get to Big House, go climb up on the platform. I will sneak away and try to find out who it is."

The Big House structure stood on a three to four foot platform that allowed access to all sides. The roof of this tiny building lay half in ruins; the years had not treated it well. Not quite as gray in color as most Mayan ruins, the front of the building was less then twenty feet across with small wooden gates that blocked the two small doorways.

Woodson, Pedro, and Blue climbed the narrow stairway to the platform while Angel quickly made his way to the opposite side of the building. Once out of sight, Angel disappeared into the jungle. Woodson and the others acted unaware of the old shaman's disappearance, when the jungle was suddenly disturbed by the sound of a single gunshot.

"Quick, get behind the temple and stay down!" Woodson yelled, as he pulled Blue and Pedro behind the stone structure.

"What's going on?" screamed Blue. "I didn't sign on to get shot at!"

"Just stay down. Pedro! Are you okay?"

Pedro signaled that he was.

"Hola, my friends," said the now familiar voice. "I see we meet again. Come out from there and see your old friend, Roberto!"

Woodson nodded to the others and they followed him around the building to face their assailant. Roberto stood about ten feet from the steps that led up to the narrow platform.

"There was another. Where is the old man?" demanded Roberto.

"The bullet must have ricocheted off the building. He's out cold and bleeding. We need to get him some help fast," said Woodson seriously.

Roberto folded his arms across his chest.

"No problem, Señor Woodson," said Roberto. "All you need to do is hand over your backpack and you can get all the help you need. I do not wish harm to anyone else."

Woodson, Pedro and Blue stood stone faced as they

watched Angel sneak up behind Roberto; the old man was carrying a large, shiny shovel.

"Here, you can have it," said Woodson, as he held out the bag containing the cylinder and his notes. "We have no further use for it."

"No tricks Woodson. Your little friend Pedro is where I can see him this time. So if you would be so kind as to hand it over—slowly."

"Here you go," said Woodson as he started to toss his bag toward, Roberto.

"Good choice, my friend," laughed their assailant. "Now, I won't have to shoot you."

"You know, Roberto," began Woodson calmly, still holding the bag, "I warned you once before about playing with guns. You just might get hurt." Woodson watched, as Angel, who was now just behind Roberto, was getting into position to strike.

"Not this time," Roberto laughed again. "I—"

Just then, Angel hit him squarely on the head with the back of the shovel. There was a loud thud. Roberto staggered, then looked squarely at Pedro.

"How?" he mumbled, just before passing out.

Pedro jumped down from the temple platform and kicked the dropped gun away from the fallen man.

"Muy bueno, Grandfather, I couldn't have done better myself. Do you think he's dead?"

"I did not hit him so hard, Pedro. He will live for you to hit him again another day, I promise," said Angel, with a playful smile.

"Doesn't this guy ever get tired of getting whacked in the head?" laughed Blue shaking her head.

"Well, gang, I think we might learn a little bit more about our friend, Aguilar, when this guy comes to," said Woodson as he jumped down from the platform.

CHAPTER TEN

News of Aguilar

"Woody, we need to talk," said Angel

"Can it wait? Roberto should be coming to any minute, and I want to know more about this guy, Aguilar."

Angel spoke slowly; there was great concern in his voice.

"Si, which is what I was starting to tell you before Roberto arrived! I know about this man Aguilar."

Woodson had no doubt that his old friend was serious.

"Okay, Angel! Take it easy and tell us."

"This Aguilar, who is chasing you, is said to be related to the Aguilar from the time of the Conquest," began Angel nervously. "He is a most serious man who has come here to find the secret of eternal life. He believes that his ancestor, Aguilar, had found a codex that contained information needed to achieve immortality."

"He believes this?" Pedro asked in disbelief.

"I'm afraid so, Pedro."

"How do you know this?" asked Woodson.

"Aguilar himself has told me!"

"What—?" gasped Pedro.

Angel nodded.

"Some time ago, Aguilar came to the resort as a guest. One night, he came to my restaurant for the late seating. As the meal ended, he offered me one hundred American dollars if I would sit and talk with him. Aguilar said that he had some questions regarding Mayan legends and history."

"Why you, Grandfather?" asked Pedro.

"You know that my knowledge of the Maya is better than anyone on this island. Others know this as well, and I am not hard to find. When we started, the conversation seemed harmless enough, and his questions were no different than most others I have been asked. But then—he went in another direction. He wanted to know about Guerrero and Aguilar. Finally, he got around to asking about the existence of a mysterious codex."

"What did he want to know?" asked Woodson.

"He wanted to know about the burning of Mayan writings at Tulum. I knew nothing of any specific times of Mayan writings being destroyed, and I told him so. Then, Aguilar became very angry. He raised his voice, questioning everything that I had told him. He acted as if I were hiding something."

"What did he do then?" asked Blue.

"He spoke of the time during the Conquest that

Bishop De Landa and his ancestor burned Mayan writings at the steps of El Castillo in Tulum. Again, he asked if I knew of such a thing taking place."

Woodson sat on the narrow steps and pulled the translations from his pack. Quickly thumbing through them until he found what he was looking for.

"The vision. That must have been Guerrero's vision. Go on."

"Aguilar again spoke of the codex. A codex, his ancestor did not burn. One that he believed had magical powers. The old Aguilar could not bring himself to destroy this codex."

"Well, that explains why he would want Guerrero's journal," began Woodson. "He must think that it could lead him to the codex. But why would he tell you? It just doesn't make sense. How could he possibly know about the journal?"

"I do not know, my friend. That is as much as he would tell me."

"Uh... Maybe," began Pedro, as he leaned over to check on Roberto, "Aguilar went to Akumal. Isn't that where Guerrero's children settled? At least that's what I learned in school. Isn't it possible that somebody there knew of these writings?"

"Pedro's right," said Woodson, "That's where I would go if I wanted to know about Guerrero!"

Just then, Roberto began to come back to life. He sat up slowly, and rubbed his head.

"Who hit me?" he asked as he looked at Angel. "Didn't I shoot you?"

"Maybe just a little, Señor," replied Angel sarcastically.

"Okay, Roberto, where's Aguilar?" demanded Woodson.

"If I tell you, will you let me go?" bargained Roberto.

"We're going to hand you over to the police either way, so you might as well tell us. If you do, we might put in a good word for you!"

Roberto hesitated.

"Okay. I will tell you all that I know," he sighed.

"That's better," said Woodson.

"He is a master of disguise. Even if you know what he looks like, you won't recognize him," said Roberto.

"Do you know where he is?" pressed Woodson.

Roberto shook his head.

"He may still be on the island. I only know that he wants your translations of whatever is in that cylinder."

"Why?"

Roberto shook his head again.

"All I know is that he hired me to follow you and bring the translations to him."

"Where did you last see him?"

"On the ferry, yesterday."

"I bet he's still in Cozumel, Woody," cried Pedro.

Woodson nodded to his young friend.

"Pedro, you come with me. Angel, keep an eye on

our friend Roberto. Blue, please keep a lookout for the security guard."

"Don't worry about him, Señor Woodson," said Roberto, "I tied him up."

"Thanks," said Woodson, as he raised an eyebrow at Roberto. "There might be hope for you yet. C'mon Pedro, we have work to do!"

"What are we going to do, Woody?" asked Pedro.

"Hopefully find another message from Guerrero!"

Woodson and Pedro climbed the narrow steps to the platform and carefully removed the short wooden gate that blocked the entrance. Once inside, Woodson took a flashlight and a brush from his bag. Handing the light to Pedro, Woodson dropped to his knees by the east wall of the temple and pointed along the floor.

"Pedro, shine the light just along the floor. That's it, just like that."

As Pedro moved the light slowly along the floor, Woodson carefully brushed the dust away, hoping to reveal another message from the past. Once they had completed inspecting the floor, Woodson took a small stone and scratched the wall a foot above the floor. Woodson instructed, Pedro to run the light across the wall at that level. By repeating this, over time they systematically went over every inch of all four walls. Still they found nothing.

"I was so sure that this was the place Guerrero would leave a clue!" Woodson sighed.

"Maybe it's outside. Maybe he didn't leave one at all. I mean, how can you be so sure?" Pedro carelessly pointed the flashlight toward the ceiling.

In the darkness, Woodson's eyes were drawn to the beam of light.

"That's it, Pedro! The ceiling! Guerrero was much taller than the average Maya." Woodson touched the ceiling. "He could have easily reached the ceiling."

Carefully, Pedro ran the light along the ceiling just ahead of Woodson's brush. Little by little the ages of dust were swept away by the archeologist's trained hands. They worked slowly, being careful not to miss one inch of the rocky surface. Pedro was amazed at the skill that Woodson worked with.

"You've got to teach me how to do that, Woody—"

"Bingo!" exclaimed Woodson brushing vigorously. "It's here, Pedro! It's here!"

The young assistant's jaw dropped as the small drawing, etched in the dark stone, became visible. He recognized the drawing instantly.

"Isn't that Tulum, Woody?" he asked,

"Absolutely!" replied Woodson.

We arrived at the City of Walls by midday. The sun was directly overhead and the heat grew intolerable. My sons were growing weak from the oppressive heat and my wife again suffered from her illness. As we walked through the village leading to the city, the women and children ran to greet us. They were carrying cool water and the familiar chowder made from maize. We rested for a time in the shade before entering the city, enjoying the hospitality of the villagers.

Once refreshed and our strength renewed, we made for the city. We could see the high walls that protected the city within. We were led to an entryway guarded by two fierce warriors armed with spears. Our guides handed them a square of deerskin and we were allowed to proceed. The wall was nearly as tall as two men and built of large rocks fitted together tightly.

As we passed through the gate, we discovered that the wall possessed even more girth than height. The path that led through this monstrous wall was not straight. You could not see the opening to the city as you entered.

We cautiously weaved through this uneven entrance; I could see the look of concern on the faces of my family and our trusted guides. Finally we exited the gate into the city and everything changed. We could smell and feel the most wonderful breeze coming from the sea. It filled our lungs with fresh air and our minds with hope.

Before us lay a city with no equal in the region. There, at the top of a hill, was a large, blue templ, surrounded by many small, brightly colored buildings. Below this was the busy marketplace filled with merchants and traders, all selling and buying wares.

We were taken to the large temple that the Spaniards now call El Castillo, to meet with the High Priest, the leader of this city. I was amazed to see that this temple, and other buildings, seemed to grow, as if alive, right from the cliff above the white sandy beach and the wonderful blue water of the sea.

The High Priest must have been expecting our arrival for he immediately asked of the mysterious book we had carried with us. Zazhal ab summoned for our guides, who had been waiting just outside with the children. She asked them to bring in the sacred writings, which she unwrapped from the deerskin covering. Then kneeling before the High Priest, she laid them neatly at his feet. The High Priest approved. Smiling, he helped my wife to her feet and summoned two women to escort us to a small hut to rest and refresh ourselves. Zazhal ab was told that we must wait until called upon again.

While waiting for our next audience with the High Priest, we explored this wonderful city. The children played near the water as my wife and I sat on the sandy shore. We wondered if this was the lost city we were to settle in.

Finally, after many days we were summoned to the temple to meet with the High Priest. It seems that the city's scholars needed more time to study the writings that we had brought with us. They decided that it was not safe for us to keep them, that we should leave the writings with them. When we protested, it was explained that this book possessed great evil. If it should fall into the wrong hands, it could destroy all balance in the world, and anger the Gods.

We were told that this book contained secrets to the Sak-Bak-Nakan, or the opening to the Otherworld of Xibalba. The Maya believe that there are two cycles of life occurring at the same time. The first deals with adventures on the face of the earth, with human beings, the other with an underworld region known as Xibalba or "Place of Fear", where the dead reside. As I was made to understand, if these cycles were made to cross or exist at the same time, the aboveground episode may alternate with the Otherworld below to enable the dead to exist on the aboveground again. What I think this means, is it might be possible to raise Gods, or people back from the underworld, or the dead, to exist on the face of the earth once again. Did this mean immortality? I did not know. I could not possibly understand.

Since this was far more than we could comprehend, Zazhal ab and I decided it would be best to leave the writings with the High Priest and his scholars. We were then instructed to rest and prepare for the last part of our journey. We had hoped that this was the lost city where we were to live, but it was not to be.

We spent the rest of our time in this place, resting for our journey. One morning, as I walked by the water, my wife came to me. She held a small piece of deerskin with images printed upon it. As I read, with her assistance, my heart warmed. It was news of the Spaniards. A Spaniard had been rescued from the jungle and brought to the safety of Cuzamil. Aguilar had made it. He was safe for now, and this made me happy.

Gonzalo Guerrero
As translated by R. Woodson

CHAPTER ELEVEN

The Lost City

"You see, Pedro, Guerrero didn't let us down. But what does this mean?" Woodson was beside himself. He was now pacing back and forth in the small dark temple. Pedro could hear him mumbling quickly under his breath.

"Woody! Are you telling me that you don't know?" Pedro asked, grabbing his mentor's arm. "Hold still, you're making me nervous."

Woodson stopped moving.

"Sorry, Pedro," he replied.

"What do we do now?"

Woodson went back to the drawing. With brush in-hand, he cleaned more of the dirt away. Suddenly, he stopped and gazed up at the musty ceiling.

"Pedro!" he exclaimed. "Move the light closer."

Pedro let out a long sigh, shrugged his shoulders and did as Woodson asked.

"Good, good. Now move along there a little bit more. That's it, stop!"

"C'mon, I'm getting hungry. I haven't eaten yet and I—"

"Patience my young friend, if you're going to be an archeologist you must learn patience." Woodson shot the boy a smile. "What do you see here?"

"It looks like Cozumel," observed Pedro.

"Look closely. Here's the sketch of Tulum," Woodson quickly brushed more dirt away, "and here are lines leading to the island and back again."

"Then he must have gone back to the mainland," said Pedro.

"It looks that way. It means that Guerrero made a round trip. But in what order?" Woodson yelled out the doorway to Blue and Angel, "I think you guy's had better get in here. Pedro, get the tracing materials."

Angel got there first. When Woodson showed him the drawings, Angel gave his friend a big hug and said, "This is amazing. I cannot believe that no other person had seen this before."

"Because they weren't looking for it," said Pedro. "But Woody knew exactly what he was looking for all along."

Woodson patted his young apprentice on the back then pointed toward the symbols that were etched into the ceiling.

"Take a tracing from here to here, and make sure you get as much of these lines as possible. Now, what do you say we free the guard, turn our friend Roberto over to the police, then sit in the shade and rest awhile? Then we'll head over to the wild side of the island for some lunch on the beach at Playa Chen Rio, and try to figure this out—my treat."

"Sounds great," said Blue, "I'm hungry. But then what? What about these drawings?" she asked

"All we can do at this point is to continue translating Guerrero's writings. The drawings only prove that the text is real. That's why I needed to find them. I wanted proof that we had the real thing. There is no question in my mind that Guerrero actually wrote them."

In the months spent in this wonderful city by the sea, waiting for our departure to the lost city that was to become our new home, I grew to love the people of Tulum. The square was always filled with merchants with the exotic wares that they sold or bartered. There were always many travelers and traders walking about telling stories of great wars and kings. Women stood at fires and prepared tortillas and chili peppers for the children as they played.

El Castillo, sitting high above the square, seemed a fitting backdrop for this city. Of the Temples I came to see in this land, none was more spectacular. From the shore, it seemed to literally

rise from the sea. But, from the square it looked more like a large friend and protector. With its long staircase leading up to the temple's three entryways, it appeared to smile lovingly over the people who built it.

The people of Tulum were preparing for Poc'am, a yearly festival that celebrates the coming of the second month of the year. All the buildings were decorated with bright colors of blue, red and white. Long thin banners shook wildly in the breezes blowing in from the sea. The sound of horns, made from conch shells, filled the air. I have yet to see a city so alive. The people here were happy and prosperous. I truly did not want to leave, but it was our destiny to live somewhere else.

Soon the day came for us to depart. Much to my surprise, the next leg of our journey was not to be by land. Rather, it was by canoe. At first, I thought we were to head south along the coast. I had heard from travelers that there were small villages along the coast where we would be safe, but never had I heard of any city of mystery that existed in that direction.

After a small ceremony at the temple and many sad farewells, we took our meager belongings and walked to the shore where our large wooden canoe waited patiently for our arrival. It was sitting with half of its dark knotted hull dug into the white sandy beach and the other half rocking gently in the brilliant blue sea. Our guides and protectors, who had brought us here, helped my family into the canoe and bade us farewell. They were to return to the father of Zazhal ab and report that we had made it this far. I do not know why they were not to travel the rest of the way. But I believe because of their devotion to us, they would have, had they been allowed.

As our ship's men pushed the canoe away from the shore, I could see the fear and uncertainty in the faces of my family. My sons did not cry. This made me proud, but I knew of nothing that could be said that would possibly ease their minds. As always, Zazhal ab was our strength and inspiration. She was able to make them smile as she pointed at the fish that came playfully to the surface.

She told the children that they had come to see us off to our new home.

The sea was clear that day. We could see the dangerous reefs that our new guides and protectors needed to navigate to bring us safely to deeper water. I looked back to see Tulum. El Castillo shined bright above the dark cliff below. And slowly, with every stroke by the oarsmen, we were carried further and further away from what we knew and closer to what we did not. We hoped this would be the end of our long journey. Home!

Our small canoe had left the shore far behind. We made our way out into the open sea where the sky and the water met in an endless tangle of blue.

After many hours of rowing against difficult currents, I finally saw what appeared to be a body of land. With the sun setting directly at our back, I knew it could be only one place. Cuzamil!

Why here? There was no lost city here. I remember the city where we visited the temple Ixchel and the many small villages that ran up and down the island. The Spanish were here. I began to feel *betrayed. I could not believe that we were being delivered into the hands of the very people we were to escape from! Zazhal ab sensed my agitation and reached out for my hand to reassure me that all was well. She spoke of Ixchel, the lunar goddess of birth and fertility and spoke of how, because Ixchel gave us three strong sons, we were now under her protection. Ixchel would never let any harm come to them or us. Still, I searched my mind. Why Cuzamil?*

Gonzalo Guerrero

As translated by R. Woodson

CHAPTER TWELVE

Aguilar Again

The seaside restaurant, at Playa Chen Rio, was still quiet at eleven thirty in the morning. The tourists from the resorts and cruise ships docked at San Miguel had not yet found their way to this beautiful windward side of the island. The natives of Cozumel call this The Wild Side. There are very few signs of human life on this side of the island. An occasional surfer riding in on a big wave and a few serious sun worshippers dot the beautiful secluded beaches to commune quietly with nature. The waves crashing the shore leave the air filled with a constant spray of salt and the smell of the open sea. The low-lying brush jungle kisses the rocky beach, filling the air with an aromatic scent of tropical plants and flowers. As you travel down the narrow road that runs along the coast, there is never a problem in finding a private spot to take it all in. There are a few restaurants along this rugged yet inviting coast and the diamond in this rough was always Pedro's favorite—the restaurant at Playa Chen Rio.

At Chen Rio's, the tables sit on the beach only a few feet away from shore. Covered by palapas, an umbrella like structure made from dried palm grass lashed together, the tables have a magnificent view of the sea.

As they enjoyed their meal, Pedro noticed a bearded man sitting at another table close by. This character seemed to be very interested in their conversation.

"Woody," whispered Pedro, "the man at the table to your left seems really interested in what we're talking about."

"You noticed it too?" replied Woodson quietly.

Pedro nodded.

"Don't say anything to your grandfather or Blue, just play along with my lead. Okay?" said Woodson, being careful not to let the others hear.

Pedro nodded again

After they finished their meal, Woodson pulled the cylinder from his bag and laid it on the table.

"Pedro," he said loudly, "in all the excitement we never fully translated the writings and figures on the cylinder, did we?

"What do you mean Woody?" replied Pedro, hoping that this was the right thing to say.

"How could we overlook this? For all we know this jar could have all the answers," he said, speaking loudly enough for the stranger at the nearby table to hear. "Maybe we've been wasting our time with the contents!"

"But I thought that—" responded Pedro but

Woodson quickly interrupted him.

"How could we be so shortsighted and leave out, possibly, the most important piece of the puzzle?" he asked, still raising his voice.

"What's gotten into you, Woody?" inquired Blue, while looking around the beach. "Don't you think, we should keep, our voices down?"

Woodson held the cylinder away from the table, and the shade of the palapa. Held in the midday sun, the faded drawings quickly came to life. As he gazed at it, his eyes wandered toward the bearded man at the other table. The man seemed most interested in Woodson and the cylinder.

"What is it, Woody?" asked Blue with a look of concern.

Woodson pretended to lose interest in the cylinder, and rubbed his chin with the back of his hand.

"Do you think I need a shave, Blue? Wouldn't I look more distinguished with a beard?"

"What are you talking about, Woody?" asked Blue, who by now had figured that Woodson had gone mad.

"You know, like that gentleman over there," he replied, pointing toward the man at the next table.

"Stop it; you're embarrassing that man and me for that matter. What has gotten into you?" demanded Blue, starting to feel more than a little uncomfortable.

"What about you, Angel?" asked Woodson, as he pointed over the old shaman's shoulder. "What do you think of that man's beard?"

Angel, who had his back to the man, slowly turned around. Just then the man jumped from the table and ran across the beach in the direction of the road. Angel leaped to his feet, as if to give chase, but as he did, he felt Woodson's firm grip on his arm.

"That was Aguilar! I'm sure of it!" exclaimed Angel.

Pedro jumped to his feet as well.

"I'll get him, Woody!"

"Just hold on, Pedro," said Woodson calmly. "We have much more to do before we deal with him. He knows that we're on to him. He's the one who needs to be careful now."

"But Woody—"

"Sit down, Pedro."

Angel motioned for Pedro to take his seat, and then sat down as well.

"That's better," said Woodson. "Now, would anyone like dessert?"

Our life in Cuzamil was very happy. My sons grew to be men, and my wife became more beautiful with every passing day. To my surprise, we have been safe here in this small city that rests in the dense jungle in the north. The Spanish have all but abandoned Cuzamil. Months had passed since the fleet had sailed to the North, into what they call the Gulf. They left for Tenochtitlán, to fight the Aztecs. I had heard the Aztecs were defeated; now, no more than slaves. The Spanish would now turn their full attention on the Maya, my people.

The elders were quite convinced that whatever happened on the mainland would not affect our life on Cuzamil. Our city was small and well hidden in this jungle. Kin, the father of Zazhal ab must have been able to see into the future to pick such a safe place for us to hide. This was indeed a lost city, for the Spanish have all but forgotten or do not care that it even exists

We indeed felt safe in our island haven, but somehow, I knew, deep inside, our perils were far from over.

Gonzalo Guerrero
As translated by R. Woodson

"Well, Blue, it's just about time to meet up with Lyons. What do you say? Can you pull yourself off that lounge chair so that we can get to San Miguel in time?"

Blue woke up to the sound of the surf and shaded her eyes so that she could see the sun as it began its soft descent to meet the sea. She sat up and stretched. Woodson just sat and smiled as he watched her come back to life.

"This is the first chance we've had to relax, Woody! Between all the traveling, translating and being chased by the bad guys, I'm exhausted. Besides, if we leave now, we'll miss a spectacular sunset."

"You can watch it from the cab. C'mon."

As they left the beach, Woodson noticed that they were again being watched. Walking along the pool, he could see an unfamiliar face casually watching them over an open book. He knew immediately that it must be Aguilar, in yet another disguise.

"Guess who's here at the resort, Blue?" asked Woodson sarcastically.

"What now?" sighed Blue.

"I think that man by the pool is Aguilar. Don't look!"

"How in the world can I see him if I don't look? Geez, you can really be a pain!"

"Go to your room and change. I need to find Pedro. He can keep an eye on this guy while we're with Lyons. I'll meet you in the lobby in fifteen minutes."

"How am I supposed to get ready in fifteen minutes?"

"Fifteen minutes, Blue!"

"Okay, okay, I'll be there. What's the matter, your shorts on too tight?"

"Go!"

The twenty-minute cab ride to San Miguel was uneventful. Blue said very little and stared out the window, trying to enjoy the beautiful sunset. Finally, with a sigh, she snapped out of her silence.

"Do you really think Lyons can help us?"

"I'm not sure. But he has been a trusted friend and mentor for some time."

"I just want someone to stop Aguilar from killing us!"

Woodson smiled and leaned toward the driver, telling him to pull over at the next street.

"I thought we were going to La Mission?" asked Blue.

"We are, but I thought that maybe we should walk a few blocks. You know, to work up an appetite."

"Oh brother!" she replied.

The cab pulled up to the corner and they stepped on to the curb. Woodson paid the driver before starting down the narrow street clogged with tourists from the numerous cruise ships that drop anchor in San Miguel on a daily basis.

"Careful, Blue. First seating for dinner is in about thirty-minutes. These folks may just knock you over on the way back to their ships."

Woodson grabbed her hand and pulled her to the safety of a small side street, heading east along the main shopping area. There were less people on this street and they were able to walk without much disturbance, except for an occasional shop owner standing on the sidewalk selling his merchandise.

As they approached La Mission, Woodson stopped dead in his tracks and pulled Blue into the doorway of one of the shops.

"Now what?" she snapped.

"Does that car look familiar?" he said, pointing at a large, black limousine parked in front of the restaurant.

"Okay! A big black car... big deal. I'm sure there are big black cars everywhere. C'mon Woody, I'm hungry."

"That's the car we had the run in with on the way back to Playa del Carmen," said Woodson, ignoring her comment. "I think that Lyons is up to his neck in this."

"Woody, you're scaring me now!"

"Yeah, I'm getting a little scared myself. Look, when we see Lyons, act like you didn't see the limo. Remember, we're just so glad to see him because we need his help."

"Got it!"

"Okay, let's go in!"

"What are you doing, Pedro, trying to scare the guests away?" asked Angel as he discovered his grandson sneaking around the resort's upstairs lobby, wearing dark glasses, a flowered shirt and a large brimmed straw hat.

"Shush," Pedro hissed. "Woody told me to keep an eye on that guy over there." Pedro pretended to point nonchalantly in the direction of the bar, where a small round figure sat comfortably sipping on a margarita.

Angel glanced questionably at the man at the bar then back at his grandson.

"What's with the getup, Pedro? You look like a silly touristo!" Angel laughed as he turned to give the man at the bar another look. "Que?" said Angel as he pulled Pedro out of sight of the man at the bar.

"What's wrong?" asked Pedro, quickly pulling off the dark glasses.

"That's him!" exclaimed Angel.

"That's who?" replied the confused Pedro.

"Aguilar!"

Pedro put the dark glasses back on and peaked around the plant to get a better look.

"Can't be, the guy at the beach looked much taller!"

"Believe me, Little One, that's Aguilar!"

"Please don't call me that," protested Pedro. "Somebody might hear you."

"Oh, sorry Pedro, I keep forgetting that you are a grown man now," snapped Angel, as he affectionately squeezed his grandson's shoulders.

"Look, the bartender just handed him a phone," gasped Pedro. "I've got to hear what he says. It might be important."

"Wait," protested Angel, tightening his grip on the young man's shoulders. "Aguilar's a dangerous man!"

"But, Woody said—"

"I know, Pedro. I will help you. Here's what we will do!"

La Mission restaurant opened to the street with a large doorway that led into the dining room. The lights were very low, with only a single, small candle to light each table. Woodson scanned the room looking for Lyons. Finally, turning to the right, he could just make out Lyons sitting at a small table in the corner in front of reproductions of Mayan ruins. Slowly, they approached the table. Lyons stood holding out his hands to greet them. Woodson wasted no time getting right to the topic at hand.

"We need your help. There is some guy named Aguilar tailing us and we don't know why. Do you know anything about this guy or what he might want?"

Lyons sat back for a moment pondering the question.

"You know, Woody, if you told me more about what you found at Tulum, it might be a help."

"Okay, maybe you should know what this is all about." Woodson began relating all that had happened during the last few days. When he finished, he sat back and waited for Lyons' response.

"Very interesting," said Lyons, as he sat back in his chair. "You know, you should really hand the cylinder and the translations over to me. You're in over your head on this one, mister. I know for a fact that the authorities have gotten word of this and are probably looking for you right now."

"How do you know about translations? I just told you that I found something. I never told you what it was, or that I had translated the darn thing!"

"Maybe he's right," interrupted Blue. "Maybe we should just give this thing up and get out of here."

"Listen to Blue, Woody," began Lyons, "I can help you, but only if you work with us."

"Us? What us? Who's us?" demanded Woodson.

Lyons answered with a distinct hesitation in his voice.

"Why, the university, of course."

"Of course," Woodson agreed sarcastically. "Look, all I wanted from you was some help in figuring this thing out. You know a lot more than you're letting on, Professor."

"C'mon, Woody," said Lyons forcing a smile. "We're old friends. Why would I try to fool you?"

"How did you know Pedro and I were coming to see you at Chichén Itzá?"

Lyons hesitated again.

"I didn't—"

"I heard you signaling the guards as we walked up the steps to the old chamber."

"But Woody—"

"I don't want to hear any more crap about you wanting to help us. There is something going on here, and I want to know what it is. Who are you working for?"

Just then, two men that were sitting at the next table stood up and moved quickly behind, Woodson and Blue's chairs. Woodson recognized the pair as the ones driving the limo. He started to stand, but two strong hands planted firmly on his shoulders pinned him down. Lyons stood up and leaned on the table with clenched fists.

"Uh-oh," said Blue, turning to Woodson.

"No more fooling around, Woody," began Lyons, "I'm not kidding. I want that cylinder and the translations, now!"

Woody looked up at his captor. He was tall with a round brown face, small, dark eyes and an evil smile revealing a front tooth made of gold.

"Where did you dig up the goons, Lyons? Or did Aguilar send them?" Then looking back up at the goon holding him down, "Nice tooth, you really do have to give me the name of your dentist."

Blue quickly leaned forward and slipped away from the man behind her. Moving so fast that the goon couldn't react, she grabbed a glass of water from the table throwing the contents in his face. Then, turning back towards Lyons, she punched him square in the jaw, knocking him back into his chair. Woodson grabbed a fork and stabbed the man behind him in the hand. The goon lost his grip allowing Woodson to stand and lunge for the man nearest Blue. Woodson laid him out with one punch. The man fell backwards, crashing onto the next table. Turning his attention to his own goon, who was busy wrapping his bleeding hand with a napkin, Woodson picked up his chair and brought it down hard on the man's head. The goon went down in a flash crashing into another table, tipping it over, spilling plates and silverware onto the floor.

Woodson grabbed Blue and rushed for the door. Running down the street, they could hear Lyons screaming at the two fallen men to get up and go after them.

"Now what?" cried Blue, gasping for breath.

"Let's head for the square. Here, down the walkway. Quick!" he replied.

From the quiet street behind they could hear the sound of squealing tires. The big black limo, they had seen before, screeched around the corner, giving chase. Woodson stopped to look back, grabbed Blue tighter and started running for the square.

"I guess they don't care that you can't drive on the walkway," yelled Blue.

"Shut up and run!" replied Woodson, gasping for breath.

The black limo began to gain on them as they approached the square. The square was a large area surrounded by shops and restaurants that rose slightly above the pedestrian walkway. As the limo exploded into the walkway and headed toward the square, Woodson pulled Blue toward the steps that led up to the plaza. People were running and diving everywhere to avoid the speeding vehicle as it neared the square. Woodson threw Blue over the steps and onto the hard stoned floor of the square just as the car approached. Woodson leaped over the short wall, barely avoiding the limo as it came to a sudden crashing stop into a small stone fountain at the end of the square. Sprawled out next to Blue, Woodson quickly sprang to his feet and pulled her up from the ground.

"We'd better get to the Ferry Landing and hail a cab." As they turned the corner, they could hear Lyons screaming at his goons again to give chase. Suddenly another vehicle squealed into the square.

"Quick get in!" shouted a familiar voice.

"Angel?" shouted Woodson, seeing his old friend in the passenger side of the Jeep.

"Get in! Get in!" cried Angel.

Woodson ushered Blue into the back seat.

"Pedro?" he said, looking at the driver. "What are you two—?"

"Are you two okay?" asked Pedro.

"Yeah—we're okay! Let's get out of here before they see us!" said Woodson as he patted his young apprentice on the shoulder.

Forced back into the seat as Pedro stepped on the gas, Woodson braced himself for a wild ride. Blue instantly fell into his arms and held on tight. Woodson could feel her tremble.

"That was fun," she said continuing to hold on tight. "If we make it through this alive, remind me to kill you, okay?"

"At least we know Lyons is definitely not going to help us," joked Woodson.

"You figured that out all by yourself, huh?" she replied.

"Hey! Where did you learn to punch like that? You nearly knocked Lyons out cold. That was great!" laughed Woodson.

"Oh, just shut up and hold me. I'm still shaking, you big dope!"

Woodson pulled her closer and tipped her head up so that he could look into her blue eyes. He smiled and placed his hand gently on the back of her head, kissing her on the forehead and nose. Then he pulled her even closer, softly kissing her lips.

"Kissing at a time like this?" cried Pedro, as he glanced into the mirror.

"Keep your eyes on the road, Little One!" exclaimed Angel.

CHAPTER THIRTEEN

Visions

Once back at the resort, Woodson and Blue settled in at the Italian restaurant for a quiet dinner. Angel broke all the rules and set up a special table in the back of the restaurant for his friends. With romantic music playing, a bottle of wine, and the tall candles on their table flickering as the evening breeze swept through the room, they hoped for a nice, long, relaxing meal.

"What do we do about Lyons?" Blue inquired, as she held up her glass for Angel to pour the wine.

"Si, what else can I do to help?" added Angel, as he turned to fill Woodson's glass.

"Enough already," pleaded Woodson. "Can't you two just leave it alone for a couple of hours? I do not want to hear one more word about Guerrero and this mess we're in. Now, if it's possible, can we just eat our dinner in peace, please?"

Angel looked at Blue, and shrugged. She sat back and sipped her wine, and pretended to stare off into space.

"Thank you," said Woodson.

Woodson had just brought the glass of wine to his lips, when Pedro burst into the restaurant and rushed to his side. Pedro was so excited he could hardly contain himself.

"Woody, we need to talk!" he exclaimed

"Not now, Pedro," Woodson said with a sigh. "It's been a tough night... Blue and I are just trying to have a nice quiet dinner."

"Muy importanté, Woody, muy importanté," prodded Pedro.

"Uh, oh, this must be important, the kid's speaking Spanish." Woodson noted to Blue with a chuckle. "Calm down, son, you're making the other guests nervous."

"Sorry, but I think you'd better come back to the room. I translated another page of Guerrero's journal—I think you'll want to see it."

"You translated a page... by yourself?"

"What do you think," said the blushing Pedro, "I just take up space at the university?"

Woodson nodded approvingly at his young apprentice.

"What got you so excited, Pedro?" he asked.

"He takes back the Codex, Woody!" exclaimed Pedro, while yanking Woodson's arm pulling him away from the table.

"What?"

"He rescues the codex from Aguilar and Bishop de Landa at Tulum!" exclaimed Pedro.

"Pedro. The vision—that was his vision." Woodson had stood up and was pulling on Pedro's arm. "C'mon."

Blue reached out and grabbed Woodson by the hand.

"What about dinner?" she asked softly.

"Right," he replied. "Angel, will you put dinner on a tray so Blue can bring it back to the room?" Woodson started away from the table then turned around. "Oh, and Angel, please meet us back at the room as soon as you can. I—" Woodson looked proudly at his young assistant,

"—we could use your help."

Woodson and Pedro rushed for the door. The young assistant was talking a mile a minute as they passed through the door and out of sight. Angel sat down at the table shaking his head. Blue handed Angel Woodson's untouched glass of wine.

"I told you, Angel. He's never going to change... ever!"

We had lived a quiet and uneventful life on Cuzamil. It had been more than forty years since I set foot on this magical land. So many things have happened here, on this island that gave us a life without fear of the Spanish. My sons had grown to be men, strong and brave, and raised families of their own. Zazhal ab still grew more beautiful every year just as my love for her became even stronger.

I could feel the years catching up to me. My hair began to gray and my skin had become like a dark tanned hide. I was happy that I stayed with these people and that I did not return with Aguilar. I felt all was well and that I could live out my days in peace.

Then, the vision came again. So many years had passed, that I had almost forgotten. I awoke from my slumber screaming. Zazhal ab grabbed and held me until I had calmed. The vision was still alive in my brain. It was exactly as I had remembered. I could see Aguilar, and the unknown horseman riding down the hill. The old fears I had for my family's safety came rushing back and once again I felt that I needed to be cautious when in the presence of strangers.

Some weeks after I experienced the return of my past fears, news came of the Spanish in Tulum. It was said that they were destroying all the writings and codice. I remembered the codex that we had left there so many years ago and the promise that I had made to Kin, the father of Zazhal ab, to protect it from the invaders.

I planned to set out immediately for the mainland. Despite my wife's protest, my sons insisted on coming to help. I welcomed them as any proud father would.

Our large dugout reached the shore near Tulum just as the sun began to set. As we beached our craft and approached the city, we could see the light from their fires leaping into the darkened sky. The Maya around the city seemed greatly agitated and there was much movement in the square that lay before the temple. We cautiously approached the crowd in the square, there were fires burning on the sacrificial platform at El Castillo. Robed figures moved about holding up crosses and praying. I could see large codices being thrown into the fires, causing general unrest to the Maya that gathered there.

I pushed my way through the throng hoping to get a better view of what was taking place. Finally, breaking through to the front I saw the codex that I had left behind so many years ago. It was on the platform with others, waiting to take its turn in the flames. I spied a horseman on the rise to the north of El Castillo and quickly realized how I could save the codex from these devils.

I directed my two younger sons to return to our dugout canoe and be ready to make way. Then, I instructed my eldest son to attract the attention of the horseman. As he tried to engage him in a conversation, I came up from the rear and pulled him off of his horse, knocking him out. My eldest son then went to join his brothers. I quickly put on the soldier's breastplate and helmet and mounted the horse.

It had seemed a lifetime since I had ridden a horse, but somehow I managed to stay aboard. My mount reared, waving its front hoofs in the air. In a flash, man and horse started down the hill toward the fires. With the steed's hoofs thundering through the crowd, I stopped before the fire. In Spanish, I screamed at the man to stop burning the books. The robed figure stopped to look directly at me. The face I beheld was the devil himself. My God! It was Aguilar—this was my vision. At that moment, I felt my world reeling in disbelief. I quickly regained my senses, jumped from the horse and *gathered up the codex that I believed to be mine. Aguilar just stared in shock and amazement; he could not believe his eyes. Getting back onto the horse, I pointed at Aguilar and warned him that these deeds would anger the Mayan Gods and that his soul would burn in the underworld until the end of time.*

Then, horse and rider burst from the city as we made our way, without chase, to my sons and escape.

Gonzalo Guerrero
As translated by Pedro Garcia

"Nice job, Pedro!" Woodson exclaimed, while pouring over the notes. "Apparently, they are teaching you something at that university." Woodson paused to rub his eyes. Pedro was aware that the archeologist was exhausted by this entire affair. "So his vision came true. The legend of Guerrero continues to grow."

Blue picked up the journal page that Pedro had translated and held it up to the light.

"Pedro, what is this symbol here in the corner?" she asked.

"The God of the Underworld," he answered.

Woodson, hearing the conversation, immediately fixed his eyes on the symbol.

"He's right," said Woodson. "But why is it just sitting there off in the corner? This is crazy! Every time we solve one mystery another one pops up! Maybe Angel can help us when he gets here. Speaking of Angel did you bring some food? I'm starving."

"Oh brother!" said Blue, as she looked over at Woodson's dinner that had been sitting untouched for over an hour.

Later that night, Pedro woke to the sounds of Woodson struggling in his sleep.

"No! No stop!" yelled Woodson, as he threw his head back and forth.

"Woody! Wake up! Wake up!" yelled Pedro. He shook Woodson vigorously.

Half awake, Woodson finally sat up in bed; he shook his head and ran his trembling hands through his hair.

"I'm all right, Pedro... I had a bad dream." His voice was soft and shaky.

"Señor?" asked Pedro incredulously. "That was a dream?"

Woodson sat there, his face appeared gaunt and very pale.

"I had that dream again where I saw a white man and a woman in a dugout canoe, rowing away from land. Then, I saw a Conquistador on horseback, rearing up against the sunset. Then, without warning the dugout was on fire and the man and the woman in it were in flames... I could feel the flames as they engulfed their bodies!"

"Again? What do you mean again?" inquired Pedro.

"Long story Pedro. I'll explain later. Please do not tell Blue about this."

"Why?"

"You know how she worries."

Pedro sat on the edge of Woodson's bed.

"I understand. She won't hear about this from me. But I sure would like to know about the dream."

"Oh, she knows about the dream," replied Woodson. "I just don't want her to know that I had it again."

"Please tell me more about the dream," said Pedro.

Woodson lay back on his pillow and quietly told his assistant about the first time that he had experienced the horrible nightmare that had haunted him for half of his life.

"Maybe it wasn't a dream, Woody. Maybe it was a vision... like Guerrero's."

"Maybe it was, Pedro. Maybe it was," said Woodson thoughtfully. "What do you say we try and get back to sleep?"

Pedro couldn't sleep. He tossed and turned restlessly through the night waiting for the birds to signal the start of the new day. Something that Woodson had said troubled him. There was something about his friend's dream that was very— familiar.

CHAPTER FOURTEEN

Conquest

I knew that Aguilar must have recognized me at Tulum. I agonized over this for the entire journey back to Cuzamil. I also knew my old friend was most certainly my enemy once again.

He would come for me, and the codex - of that I was sure. I knew that the best action I could take would be to hide the codex. Zazhal ab agreed. But first, she felt it was necessary to read and memorize as much of the writings as possible. She took the codex to the building that is said to be of great importance in this sacred city of Ixchel, the lunar goddess of birth. There, in the shade of the thatched roof, she sat between the two large circular pillars that marked the entrance and began to decipher and memorize the writings. Over her left shoulder, I could see the mysterious red handprints on the wall. This building was *known as the Place of the Little Hands and was believed to have once been the home of the great overlord of this city. His name, I was told, was Ah Halach and legend has it that he ruled this city many centuries before. It is said that the little red handprints on the wall were believed to be his very own. A legacy, left with no doubt, to remind the many generations to come of his greatness.*

As I sat atop the ancient tomb near the Place of the Little Hands, I planned my search for a safe hiding place for the writings. I knew the temple of the lunar goddess, in the city's main square, would be the first place that Aguilar would look. I needed to locate a place that would protect these precious writings from the elements and from him. I walked from building to building, weighing all the possibilities. Then, as I realized that my task might be a futile one, I returned to the ancient tomb. Again I watched Zazhal ab as she sat there memorizing the codex. It was then I noticed that there was a step at the base of the pillar in need of repair. Quickly, I crossed over to the building and attempted to move the stone. Zazhal ab grunted with much dissatisfaction on being disturbed. I moved the stone and reached in under the pillar. To my surprise, there was a small well beneath. It was made of stone and mortar and was undoubtedly used to center the pillar when it was dropped into place. Then, after this was completed the step was probably built around it, covering up the well. It was perfect. A stroke of luck or perhaps fate! This is where I would hide the codex, under the darkness of the night so none but myself, would know.

It was less than one cycle of the moon before Aguilar came for the codex. We had been resting from our daily work and the sun was low in the sky. We had planned on leaving the city the next day for the mainland. We had friends there in a small fishing village and thought we might be safer.

As I sat resting, a figure emerged from the shadows. Relaxed, I was not ready for the blow that was to come. As I lay sprawled out on the ground, I did not need to look up to know that my attacker was Aguilar. Who else could it have been?

Aguilar cursed at me in Spanish. It was as if he was possessed. He just kept screaming threat after threat... I struggled to my knees and prepared myself for the next blow, but it did not come. He just stood over me and laughed, pointing at my tattoos and the native jewelry that I wore. At this moment, he was off guard; I grabbed some dirt and threw it into his eyes. As he brought his hands to cover his face I lunged forward, grabbed his legs and brought him to the ground. We struggled for a few moments and just as I gained the advantage, I was quickly pulled off my attacker by two strong pairs of hands. I was forced to stand by two soldiers, one on either side. They were fully armed Conquistadors, highly trained and dangerous. I struggled in vain as a third man came from behind and grabbed me around the neck.

Aguilar smiled, of my fate— there was no doubt. Again he cursed and warned me that if I did not tell him where he could find the codex, I would die. By this time, my people had gathered around. Aguilar spied Zazhal ab and pulled her from the crowd. I struggled even harder, but still *in vain. Then, as Aguilar placed his filthy hands upon her throat, I heard the sound of spears in the air and the impact as they hit their targets. I could feel the grip of my captors falter as they fell, bleeding, to the ground. My sons! They had come to our rescue! I leaped for Aguilar and felled him with one mighty blow, causing him to release my wife. As he lay there, looking at his wounded soldiers, he knew that he was beaten and that I had this day won the battle.*

Aguilar and his men were allowed to leave. I knew that this was not the end. He and I would someday resume this battle.

Gonzalo Guerrero
As translated by R. Woodson

The birds greeted the day as light from the morning sun peeked through the thickly branched trees. Woodson sat outside the room working on the translation. Sitting back in his chair, he smiled while shading his eyes from the new day's sunny glare. Guerrero's beads held tightly in his fist, Woodson knew where the codex could be found. After the elation of knowing that his search would soon come to an end, also came the realization that Blue was right. His career could be over. He could go to jail. What about his friends? He knew that he would take full responsibility for all actions in this matter and felt that should be enough to keep his friends out of trouble. But, would that be enough?

His reverie was disturbed when Pedro opened the door and stepped outside. Woodson offered a seat to his yawning apprentice and smiled. Pedro noticed the writings on the table and the beads in Woodson's hand.

"You let me sleep too late, Woody. I wanted to get up early and—"

"You might enjoy this section," Woodson sighed. "You read. I'm going to wash up."

Woodson handed the translation to Pedro and went inside the room. The young man shaded his eyes from the sun as he read the latest translations. Pedro felt the excitement well up inside. The codex—it can be found, he thought. Pedro jumped up and ran back inside the room. He found Woodson in the bathroom, standing over the sink with razor in hand.

"This is it, Woody! I can't believe it! When do we go to find it? No, no, first we need to call Angel, and then—" Pedro, who was speaking in rapid fire stopped abruptly, as Blue walked in from the adjoining room, still wearing her nightshirt.

"What in the world is all the commotion about? Can't a girl get a little shut eye?" she asked, while still rubbing the sleep from her eyes.

"Blue! Look, we know where the codex is," shouted Pedro, shoving the notes in front of her face.

Blue pulled the notes from Pedro's hand and started to read. Finally reading where the codex could be found she jabbered, "This is it! I can't believe it! When do we go? No, no. First, we need to call Angel—"

Woodson walked out into the room, wiping bits of shaving crème from his face with a towel.

"Did you guys rehearse this?" he asked.

"When are we going?" gasped Blue. "I can be ready in five minutes, I swear!"

"I'm with Blue, Woody. Let's go!" cried Pedro with delight.

Woodson sat on the edge of the bed. Still wiping his face, he stared blankly at the ceiling fan turning slowly above his head. Blue and Pedro both stood there in anticipation, waiting to hear the next move in their adventure. Finally, Woodson turned his attention back to them. He thought how beautiful Blue looked first thing in the morning, especially in that cute nightshirt. Then, he thought of Pedro and the promising future he had as an archeologist. Woodson knew that these were good people who cared for him very much. They were his family.

"How about we get some breakfast? I am really hungry!" he said, finally.

"What in blazes are you talking about, Woody? The

codex! Let's get on the road!" exclaimed Blue.

Woodson tossed his towel over his shoulder and replied, "No Blue, not this time."

"Are you okay?" Pedro inquired.

"I'm fine," sighed Woodson.

"Okay, what is going on here?" Blue snapped, her tone harsh and impatient.

Woodson stood and walked to the open doorway. He looked out at the courtyard below. Throwing his towel on the floor, he turned and put a hand on each of their shoulders.

"It's over guys. I can't put you or myself through this any longer. I'm going to turn Guerrero's writings over to the authorities and try to make the best deal I can."

Blue reached across her body and gently placed her hand on his.

"Woody, as far as we know, the authorities don't even know about this yet. You can bet that Lyons and his goons haven't told anyone and we know that Aguilar won't. So, what's the problem?"

"You... both of you, and Angel. You're my problem. Don't you understand? If I go down on this thing, you will too!"

Blue shook her head.

"We're willing to take that chance. Right, Pedro?"

"Si. We want to see this through and so does Angel," he replied.

Woodson sat down on the bed, his face cradled deeply into in his open palms; he looked over his fingers at Pedro and Blue. His friends couldn't see it through his hands but Woodson was smiling. He always knew that he could count on them, but he never realized how much.

"You know this guy, Aguilar, plays for keeps," he said, his words slightly muffled by his hands. Blue and Pedro nodded in agreement. "Lyons didn't seem too happy with us last night—either."

Blue smiled and balled her hand into a tight a fist.

"We handled him once. I think we can do it again," Blue said proudly, remembering the right hook she landed to Lyons' jaw.

"You guy's really want to do this, don't you?"

"You bet, Woody," cried Pedro.

"Look Woody," began Blue, "I've spent the last three days bouncing around the Yucatan in cars and planes. I've been chased and shot at. The worst of it is I've had to put up with you, you big dope. I have no intention of stopping now. Got it?"

Woodson stood and gave Blue a hug. He felt his confidence returning.

"It's against my better judgment, but geez, I really do want to see if that codex is there," he said. Woodson shook his head and laughed. "Hey, why not? So I spend the next ten years in a Mexican jail... Blue, you get dressed, pronto. Pedro and I will finish up here and meet you in the lobby. Hurry!"

Blue scurried to her room as Pedro hit the shower. Woodson stood in the open doorway and, again, stared out on the sun-drenched courtyard. Shutting the door, he looked down at the green beads in his hand.

"I've got a bad feeling about this."

An hour later, Woodson, Pedro and Blue arrived at San Gervasio to find what they believed would be the resting place of the codex that Guerrero referred to in his journals. When they pulled up, Angel was already waiting at the entrance

"Come on, I've already taken care of the guard," said the old shaman, as he waved them through the entrance.

"How much time, Angel?" asked Woodson eagerly.

"About an hour... maybe more; before the guides and the workers arrive."

Angel carried a pick and shovel. Handing the shovel to Pedro, Angel and his grandson fell quickly into step behind Woodson and Blue as they made their way down the rocky, muddy path to the building described by Guerrero in the journals—The Little Hands Structure.

"Which one, Woody?" asked Angel, as they arrived at the small building.

Woodson stood and carefully eyed the two round pillars that stood at the front.

"Well?" asked Blue, gesturing with her hands

palms up, pointing at the steps below the pillars.

"Just give me a minute, now. I'm thinking," replied an uncertain Woodson.

"You mean, you don't know? Mr. Archeology doesn't know which step it is?" cried Blue sarcastically.

"Look Blue," began Woodson, "Guerrero never said which one it was. I just figured that it would become apparent, which one it was, when I saw them. How was I supposed to know?" He turned to Angel. "Angel—best guess. You're the expert on this site."

"I'm not so sure either, amigo. They both look the same to me," responded Angel.

Pedro knelt down at the step in front of the pillar on the left and pointed toward the red hand imprints on the wall behind the pillar to the right.

"That one, Woody... It has to be," said Pedro confidently.

"The right one?" asked Woodson.

Pedro stood and gestured toward the painted handprints.

"The one on the right, I'm sure of it!" he exclaimed.

Woodson wiped the sweat from his brow.

"Why are you so sure?" he asked. "It could be either one."

"No! Listen!" Pedro paced back and forth in front of the steps. "Guerrero was quite clear about looking at the handprints—over Zazhal ab's left shoulder—"

"Right!" exclaimed Woodson. "Guerrero mentioned

that she grunted when he messed with the pillar... he didn't say that she moved. Pedro, I think you're on to something" Woodson took the pick from Angel and handed it to his young apprentice. "Even if you're wrong, we've still got a fifty-fifty chance. My young friend, the pleasure is all yours. The step at the base of that pillar," said Woodson pointing toward the one on the right. "If you please?"

Pedro dropped his shovel and took the pick in both hands. Raising the pick overhead, he was about to bring it down on the stone when a familiar voice shouted from the jungle.

"Stop!"

Everybody turned to see a group of men approaching. It was Lyons and the two goons.

"What do you want, Lyons?" Woodson yelled out.

"Whatever it is that you are about to find, my old friend," snapped Lyons. He smirked as he spoke.

"Why did you stop us?" asked Woodson "Why didn't you just wait until we found it and take it away then? Your friends here have the guns."

Lyons knelt over the pillar on the right and gently rubbed the crumbling stone step just beneath it.

"So this is where Guerrero hid the codex. Interesting... Well, I guess if it's there we should liberate it."

Woodson grabbed Lyons by the shirt and pulled him up. As the two men stood face-to-face, Lyon's men started toward them.

Lyons quickly held up his hand, signaling them to stop.

"I'm asking you, Lyons. Why?" demanded Woodson.

Lyons pulled himself away and pointed toward the building.

"It's because there is someone else here—someone who has the right to find the codex!"

As Lyons finished talking, the jungle fell silent. From behind the building walked an odd, portly looking figure dressed in white and wearing a large panama hat. His round face was bright red from the jungle heat, and sweat poured profusely from his shaded brow.

"Aguilar!" exclaimed Woodson.

"In the flesh, Mr. Woodson," said Aguilar, as he wiped the sweat from his brow. Then turning to Lyons, "You were right, Lyons. He does dress like that, Indiana Jones, fellow from the movies."

"All right, that's enough," said Woodson impatiently. He hated when people said that.

The small man approached Woodson and poked the archeologist on the chest with his pudgy, pink finger.

"You are a very clever man, Mr. Woodson." Aguilar paused. "Though, I must thank you for leading me to the codex."

Woodson pushed Aguilar's hand away and turned to Lyons who suddenly had trouble looking his old friend in the eye,

"So—you can be bought?"

"I guess we all have our price," said Lyons with a frown.

"Not all of us!" Woodson growled through clenched teeth. "What is this all about?"

Aguilar walked over to Pedro and attempted to pull the pick from his hands. The young man tightened his grip on the handle.

"What a brave young man," said Aguilar, "but not very bright." Aguilar motioned to one of the goons who quickly pulled a small revolver from his pocket and pointed it at the young man.

Woodson nodded and Pedro immediately loosened his grip allowing Aguilar to snatch the handle.

"That's much better." Aguilar stepped up to the pillar. "The step just below the pillar?" he asked. Pedro looked down at the ground and nodded. Immediately, with a crash, Aguilar brought the pick down onto the base of the step exposing an opening to a well directly below the pillar. Aguilar fell to his knees and reached down into the well until his right arm was completely swallowed below the great pillar. Then, slowly his arm reappeared. He struggled briefly to free the object from the well and started to laugh; a wicked, maniacal laugh.

"It's here! My God I have it now!"

CHAPTER FIFTEEN

Discovery

As Aguilar pulled the codex from the well, Woodson noticed that Lyons and his men were busy watching as Aguilar struggled to free the codex; they were no longer paying any attention to him and the others. Slowly backing away from the building, Woodson motioned for his friends to follow. Aguilar jumped up from his knees and pulled the small rectangular, dusty leather bundle close to his chest. The dirt stained his once crisp white shirt but he didn't seem to mind.

Glancing up, Aguilar quickly spied Woodson, and the others backing away.

"Please stay, Mr. Woodson. It would be a pity for you not to at least see what you have been seeking all this time."

Lyon's men immediately turned their attention and their guns toward Woodson, and the others. Woodson realized, at this point, that escape was futile. He could feel Blue's hand reach out and grab his. She had a firm grip. Woodson squeezed her just as tightly.

"Look Aguilar, or what ever your name is, let

my friends go. The only reason they're even here is because of me."

Aguilar held the codex up and looked at it with an intense longing.

"I have no intention of hurting you or your friends Mr. Woodson."

"What?"

"No, no, I don't do murder... There is no reason to kill you or your friends."

"Aren't we witnesses?" asked Blue.

"To what, young lady?" asked Aguilar enigmatically. "Mr. Woodson, or can I call you Woody? The way I see it, you are as guilty as we are."

"Professor Woodson will do," said Woodson sternly. "How do you figure that we're all guilty?"

"Did you not find something at Tulum?" inquired Aguilar sarcastically.

"Well yeah but—"

"Did you report your findings?"

"No, but—"

"Did any of you share your knowledge with the proper authorities?"

Nobody spoke.

"I thought not," continued Aguilar—confidently. "As far as the authorities are concerned, we might as well all be in this together." Aguilar turned to his men. "So if you gentlemen will please put down your guns, we can get on with the unveiling. We have less than an hour before the guides open this site to the public, so gather around."

Aguilar set the codex on the step between the pillars. Gently, he peeled away the deerskin cover that had protected the ancient writings for so many centuries.

"Why do you want this codex so badly?" Woodson interrupted Aguilar before he could open the folded pages of glyphs. "Why is it so important?"

"You don't know, do you?" asked Aguilar, who stopped unwrapping the codex, and gave Woodson an incredulous smile. "You really don't know? This is incredible. Didn't your little journal tell you?"

"It told us that the book you are about to open possesses great evil," said Pedro stepping forward.

"I must admit," began Aguilar, "your little friend here is right. Not only does this codex possess evil, but the power to use it as well!"

"How could you possibly know this?" asked Woodson.

"Tell him, Lyons!" Aguilar sighed loudly, as if he were completely disinterested.

Lyons came forward and pulled another clay cylinder from the bag he was carrying.

"Where did you get that?" Woodson asked amazed by the similarities to Guerrero's cylinder.

"Look Woody, Guerrero wasn't the only one to write about what happened during the Conquest. Aguilar did as well," said Lyons.

"And you guys just happened to find it! That's a good one," said Blue sarcastically.

"Blue!" warned Woodson.

"No Woody," began Blue, "These guys are full of it! What are the chances that this guy finds a cylinder from his great, great, great, great grandfather, or whatever, at about the same time you find Guerrero's?"

"I found this cylinder three years ago, Blue" admitted Lyons.

"You knew about it all this time and you never shared it with anybody?" cried Woodson.

"I'm afraid not, Woody." replied Lyons.

"What were you thinking of?"

"Money. What else?"

"Why?"

"My retirement is coming up, and as you will learn soon enough, an archeologist's pension just doesn't cut it."

"I am really confused, now!" Woodson exclaimed as he started to pace back and forth. "Where did you find it?"

"At Chichén Itzá, the Caracol Observatory to be exact."

Becoming increasingly bored with the ensuing conversation, Aguilar started unwrapping the codex. Woodson rushed over to his side to distract him.

"Wait, Aguilar! Before you open that thing up, I

think we'd better discuss this just a little more. What you are about to do could be dangerous. Just a couple more minutes, please!"

"You have two minutes to ask any questions you might have—then, I open it," snapped Aguilar.

Woodson turned on Lyons, the two men stood face to face.

"How did you find it?"

"By accident. I was replacing some stones that had come loose on the interior circular staircase. As I removed the stone, there it was. Bingo!"

"Did you open it and translate as I did with Guerrero's?"

"Yes, with young Pedro's help."

"Pedro?" said Woodson and Blue in unison.

"Yes, Pedro was with me when I found it."

Aguilar started to laugh. He picked up the codex and held it up to Woodson's face.

"Of course Pedro was with him. And now he works for me. Do you think that it was an accident that Pedro found Guerrero's writings at Tulum? We planted it there so you would find it."

"Why me?" pleaded Woodson.

"Lyons struggled in translating the Old Spanish in Aguilar's journal. But he did learn enough to help us find Guerrero's journal." Aguilar laughed. "It took almost three years to find but once we did, Lyons found it even more difficult to decipher then my ancestor's.

So we decided to get help with Guerrero's. Who in the region can read Mayan glyphs and old Spanish as well as you, Mr. Woodson?"

"So the whole thing was a set up. You son of a—" Woodson jumped toward Aguilar and grabbed him firmly by the collar. "What about that knucklehead, Roberto, where did he fit into all this?"

Aguilar motioned for Lyons and his men to pull Woodson away. Then, after straightening his collar he replied, "Ahh, Roberto! I hired him to follow you... though he didn't know it. He thought he was going to bring me the journal. I knew he would fail, but he did update me as to your whereabouts. He was there to keep you looking over your shoulder—to keep you from suspecting what was really going on—and to keep you curious about the writings. Curious enough, I may say, that you indeed translated enough of them to lead us all to this treasure."

"Si Woody, I am afraid that what he says is all true. But I did not know about Roberto," confessed Pedro.

Woodson wrestled his arms away from Aguilar's men.

"Okay, okay! Let's just forget about who knew what and where the writings were found. We can sort that out later." Woodson was furious. "Bottom line, Aguilar, is what on earth is so important about this codex?"

Aguilar, still holding the ancient writings, turned and handed it to Lyons.

"Sorry, Mr. Woodson, but your time is up and so is mine. Lyons, take the codex to the car. I've decided to open it later. Please, gentlemen and lady, if you would be so kind not to follow us. I do not want to see anybody harmed. Good day!"

"What about Guerrero's writings?" Lyons asked as he took the codex from Aguilar.

"They can keep them. They're of no use to me now." Aguilar turned to Pedro, "Pedro, are you coming with us?"

Pedro looked at Woodson, hoping for some sign that he could stay. Looking back at Pedro, Woodson nodded his head and smiled.

"No, Señor Aguilar, I think I will stay with my friends."

Aguilar shook his head as he, Lyons and their men walked away with The Fifth Codex.

After the incident with Aguilar and his men, I decided that we must leave Cuzamil. There are many small villages on the mainland and I felt certain that we would be safe from reprisals. In the months that followed, my family seemed even happier living in the small village of Akumal. It gave us an opportunity to grow close again.

In the back of my mind I knew that

Aguilar would come. Someday he would come. It was not over. But, at least the codex, of sacred writings, was safe from the Spaniards and that was most important.

One night I awoke to the sounds my wife crying in her sleep. I tried to wake her but I could not. Her cries grew louder and more intense with every breath that she took. I did not know what to do. Finally, after what seemed to be an eternity, Zazhal ab awoke, trembling, and covered in sweat. She held me tighter than she had ever before. She fell back into a deep sleep as she lay in my arms. I held her until the first light of morning when she finally woke.

At first, she would not speak of what she dreamt. As the days passed, she became more comfortable with letting it out. She claimed that she was now certain that the writings in the hidden codex were the work of evil. She went on and on about a Serpent Bar, a double headed snake scepter that could be a portal by which the Gods and the Mayan rulers could pass back and forth from the Underworld to our world. She *kept making these strange hand gestures by holding her wrists back to back and pointing her thumbs out. I did not understand any of what she spoke; I was terrified that Zazhal ab might have been truly possessed by an evil spirit. I knew that the only course of action would be to bring her to a shaman, a wise man who knew of all things Maya—good and evil.*

Gonzalo Guerrero

As translated by R. Woodson

CHAPTER SIXTEEN

The Chase Begins

The ride from San Gervasio was dreadfully quiet. Woodson was confused about Pedro's loyalty. Except for Blue complaining about being hungry, not one word had been spoken about what had taken place at the San Gervasio ruins.

"What were you thinking, Pedro?" asked Woodson finally breaking the silence. The young assistant had just pulled the Jeep into the parking lot at the resort.

"I thought I was helping you," said Pedro, his eyes tearing.

"Helping me!" Woodson exclaimed. "Big help you are!"

Blue reached up to the front seat and slapped Woodson on the side of his head, knocking his hat off onto his lap.

"Give the kid a chance to explain!" she scolded.

"He must have an explanation." Angel frowned at Pedro. "You do have an explanation, Little One?"

Pedro nodded stiffly, sniffing back tears.

Woodson shot a threatening glace at Blue.

"Okay, okay" he snapped. "I'll let the kid talk, but

no more hitting!"

"Unless you deserve it, you big dope," said Blue, pointing a threatening finger at Woodson.

"It was three years ago, Woody," began Pedro with a sniffle, "I was just a kid. Angel drove us out to Chichén Itzá for the day so I could watch Professor Lyons and the other archeologists while they worked. I spent the afternoon with Professor Lyons while he replaced some stones at El Caracol—"

"That's when Lyons found the old Aguilar's journals," said Woodson impatiently.

"Si, I was with him when he found it. I had no idea what he had found, but he made me promise not to tell anyone..." Pedro turned to look at his grandfather and continued, "Especially you Angel."

"Okay. Let's fast forward to the other day at, Tulum," said Woodson.

Pedro wiped away the tears that had welled up in his eyes.

"Some days before you arrived, one of the maintenance team had accidentally found the dislodged stone and immediately called Professor Lyons."

"So, you were working for me when you planted the Guerrero cylinder in Tulum. How did this come about?" asked Woodson.

"Lyons asked me to, Woody. All I was told was, that if I did this, I'd be paid a lot of money."

Angel became visibly agitated.

"So you betrayed—our friend—for a few lousy dollars. Pedro I—"

"No. It wasn't like that," protested Pedro, waving his hands, as he started to open his door.

Blue grabbed Pedro's arm and gently pulled him back into his seat.

"Just relax, we will sort this out. Go ahead and tell Woody why you did this... Woody, let him explain."

Pedro settled back into his seat and regained his composure.

"Professor Lyons asked me to take a look at the stone and report back to him. How surprised do you think I was when I found the cylinder buried behind the stone. I had found the cylinder just a few days before you arrived at Tulum. Lyons came to the site the same day. After opening it and investigating the contents, he told me that he wanted you to handle the translations. He knew that you couldn't resist knowing more about a find like this."

"So you had seen the writings first?" asked Woodson.

"Si, I even agreed that you be the one to translate—"

"That's why you stopped me from prying the cylinder open. It had already been opened and if I had attempted to open it I would have realized— Oh my god. How could I be so stupid? I was so excited I just thought that it was the passing time that caused the lid to fall off. You changed your mind. You tried to stop me from reading the darn things"

"Si!" exclaimed Pedro.

"And the stone falling on your head was staged too?"

Pedro's sundrenched face flushed with embarrassment as he nodded.

"Wait a minute... Lyons had you replace the cylinder before I arrived. He knew that I was slated to restore that wall. Then, when I was delayed in getting there, you 'accidentally' found it when I arrived. Lyons pretended to be ignorant at Chichén Itzá, but he knew I had the cylinder all along. The plan then had to include you to make it work. They're cleverer than I thought! What about Aguilar? Did you meet him?"

"No."

"So, all of your directions came from Lyons?"

"Si."

"What about our friend, Roberto?"

"I found out about him and Aguilar when you did. I never even knew about Aguilar or that Lyons was working for anybody other than the university."

"Why, Pedro? If not for the money, why would you betray our friend," Angel inquired.

"Lyons told me that he wanted you to get the credit for the discovery. He said that you were in trouble at the university and that this was just what was needed to set things right. Honest Woody, I thought I was helping you. I didn't care about the money."

Woodson jumped out of the car.

"That dirty—"

"Here he goes, again. Sit down, Woody. You're making me nervous," said Blue.

"No, Blue. I've got work to do," said Woodson, jumping from the car. Suddenly he turned back, his eyes began to light up and his mouth stretched into a huge Cheshire smile.

"You okay, Woody?" asked Blue cautiously.

"Never better, Sweetheart." then turning to Pedro, "How much of the Aguilar writings can you recall... the key parts only?"

"C'mon Woody, I was only thirteen years old when Lyons found it."

"Don't give me that. Angel has been teaching you since you were—"

"Okay, okay," replied Pedro. "I think can remember some. It was written in Old Spanish, very difficult to read. Why?"

Woodson ignored his assistant's question.

"Angel, how much time do you have before you have to go to work?"

"It's my night off."

"Perfect! Go call Pedro's grandmother and tell her you won't be home till late. We have a lot of work to do!"

Blue crawled out of the backseat.

"What are we going to do now?" she asked.

"Pedro is going to write down what he remembers of the Aguilar writings." Woodson turned to Angel, who was still seated in car. "And you, my friend, are going to interpret them. Being a shaman gives you more insight to what happened around here in the past."

"And what about me?" asked Blue.

"You are going to help me translate the rest of these writings!" he exclaimed as he placed the cylinder on the hood of the jeep and watched it roll toward Blue.

"Then what?" asked Blue, as she caught the cylinder with one hand.

"We're going to put it all together and figure out what Aguilar and Lyons are up to" declared Woodson.

"And then?" asked Blue.

Woodson brought his hand crashing down on the hood of the car, causing his friends to jump. "Stop him from carrying out whatever evil he is planning," he said dramatically.

Woodson looked at his three friends who stood there in complete silence. Blue looked at Pedro, and then at Angel, then completely ignoring Woodson, announced, "I'm starving! How about you two guys? Are you hungry, too?"

"I could eat," Pedro answered with a smile. "How about you, Angel?"

"Sure, sounds good," he replied.

"Well then, let's head to the dining room," said Blue.

Pedro and Angel joined Blue and, together, they started walking away.

"When you calm down, you're welcomed to join us, Woody," said Blue over her shoulder impatiently.

"But guys—" pleaded Woodson.

Blue turned to Woodson.

"Look, Woody, we'll get this done, but we've all had a tough morning. So... let's just relax and discuss this calmly over lunch."

"Blue!" said Woodson sternly.

The trio ignored Woodson as they headed for the dining room. Woodson stood there with his hands on his hips in utter disbelief.

"Hey, you guys," he called out, "What are you doing? Why are you ignoring me? C'mon guys, we don't have much time..."

Just then, a small boy about ten years old walked up to Woodson and tugged on his jacket.

"Hey Mister," said the little boy gazing up at Woodson.

"Yes," Woodson replied slowly—looking down at the boy—fighting the urge to smile.

"Are you that Indiana Jones guy from the movies?" asked the youngster in a high squeaky voice.

"Sorry kid, I'm afraid not," Woodson replied with a shrug. "Hey guys, wait for me," calling out after his three companions.

In the weeks that passed, Zazhal ab spent many a sleepless night. Her nightmares became more vivid with every passing day. We awaited the arrival of the shaman with great hope and anticipation. On the night before his arrival, she could not sleep; her fears had become much too great.

On that night, I had the vision of my death again. I awoke crying out in pain and covered in sweat. Even though she was exhausted from lack of sleep, my love held me and helped me through my pain.

Some hours later, as the sun began to rise, an old woman came to our hut to announce the coming of a chosen one. The shaman was shown to our hut and without so much as uttering a word, began to light fires to sticks of incense that filled our hut with an acrid smell that caused my eyes and throat to burn.

The shaman was a small, dark man whose wrinkled face spoke volumes of his age and wisdom. His clothes were from deerskin and he was adorned with many green beads.

We told him of the codex. How

my wife had committed much of it to memory and of the evil that it had brought to her. After we had told him all, he fell into a silent trance for what seemed an eternity. His breathing became deep, almost sleep-like, but his eyes remained open as if looking into emptiness.

When he awoke, he began chanting and waved the burning sticks of incense over his head. After a while, he stopped and asked where I had hidden the codex. When I told him, he seemed content that it was in a safe place where it could never be found.

He told us that what we had read from was the Mayan sacred book of the underworld, or as he put it, the book of death. The shaman explained that this book was thought to be only a legend. He seemed very troubled that it actually existed. He spoke of the legend that told of a book that could give a human being, in this world, the ability to cross over to the Underworld and back again at will, making them immortal.

We were in disbelief but he was so emphatic in this belief that I had offered to take him to the codex. Of this he declined, stating that our world and the Underworld would be so much better if it were to remain hidden for all time.

He told us that Zazhal ab's dreams would fade in time, and that she should try not to think of the evil that she had learned. Upon asking about my visions, he said with great regret, "With this, I cannot help. You must confront the one who troubles you. You are not truly of my people, but if you believe the visions to be your destiny, then it shall be." With that he left us.

For the first night in some time, my wife slept in peace. I slept very little. I kept thinking of the visions that I believe were of my death. I wondered if indeed the shaman was correct. Did I need to confront Aguilar? Would this give me peace? As the night wore on, my decision was clear.

The next morning, I explained to my wife that I had decided to travel to Tulum and find Aguilar. She of course, insisted that she accompany me. At first I protested, but after all we had been through together I could not deny her. We decided to journey to Cuzamil first *see if the codex was still safely hidden. Upon our arrival, we found the city in great chaos and despair. He had been there! The monster had returned to find the codex, leaving death and destruction in his path. Thank the gods. The codex was safe.*

An old woman came to me and handed me a scrap of paper. It was real paper from Spain. On it, written in my native tongue, were three words. COME TO TULUM.

Gonzalo Guerrero
As translated by R. Woodson

"All right gang, what have we learned from this translation?" asked Woodson as he paced back and forth on the balcony of his room. Blue, lying comfortably in the hammock, was the first to speak up.

"That we are more than likely heading for the mainland tomorrow," she said. "C'mon already, we have been at this for hours! We're missing a great sunset here."

Angel stood and leaned over the table, again glancing at the notes that he had made from his conversations with Pedro.

"Pedro only got to see about half of the old Aguilar's writing. From what I can tell, Blue's right, the answer is at Chichén Itzá. I believe that is where our Aguilar is headed."

"Si, Woody, Angel and I think Aguilar and Lyons are headed to the Sacred Cenote there," added Pedro.

"Why?"

"The Sacred Cenote is a portal to the underworld!" Pedro replied.

Woodson looked down at the red tile floor and rubbed his chin thoughtfully.

"According to what I had studied about the Cenote," he began, "It was used for human sacrifice. Men, women and children were bound and thrown into the deep well, drowned to appease the Gods. How could it possibly serve as a portal between the worlds?"

Angel and Pedro both began to answer at the same time. Angel smiled and allowed his grandson to continue.

"If you remember, Woody, if the victim for some reason survived the sacrifice, he was thought to then be a chosen one that the Gods smiled upon."

"Is it possible that this lunatic thinks that he can conjure up some special power from the codex?" asked Woodson.

"Without the codex, there is no way to know," answered Pedro. "The writings of the old Aguilar were very sketchy, but I do know this—he was seeking something evil, very evil and he needed that codex to find it."

"Well, I guess we should hit the hay so that we can get an early start for Chichén Itzá in the morning. I'll go down to the front desk and make the arrangements. I hope we're not too late," said Woodson as he headed for the stairs.

"I cannot go with you tomorrow, my friends," Angel began, "I have many things that keep me here, but my prayers go with you. You must stop Aguilar." Angel put his arm around Pedro. "And you be careful, Little One".

Pedro blushed right through his sun-darkened skin.

"Angel!" Pedro hated when Angel called him that.

"We'll call you as soon as we can" said Woodson. "Thanks for all of your help, my friend. We couldn't have gotten this far without you."

"Gracias, Woody. But remember—if you need me—I will be on the next plane. Now, come with Angel to Caruso's. I will make you the best dinner ever."

Blue jumped up from the hammock as if she were shot out of a cannon.

"Eats! What are we waitin' for? I'm starving!" she exclaimed.

"Is that all you think about, food?" asked Woodson shaking his head.

Blue smiled.

"A girl's got to eat. C'mon, Pedro let's go."

CHAPTER SEVENTEEN

Confrontation

As the morning sun peeked over the quiet jungle, Woodson began to toss and turn wildly in his bed. After a few minutes, the tossing and turning turned to thrashing and groaning. Pedro suddenly woke from a sound sleep. Still groggy, the young man sat up in his bed. Woodson appeared to be going into a near convulsive state. Pedro jumped out of bed and banged on the door to Blue's adjoining room.

"Blue! Blue! Come in here, quick," he yelled. Pedro went to the bed, grabbed Woodson by the shoulders and held him down. Blue rushed through the door; she was still putting on her robe.

"What's going on, Pedro?" she asked. "What's wrong with Woody?"

"I think he is having another vision. Help me wake him up," cried the young assistant.

"Another vision? What are you talking about?" Blue appeared confused.

"I'll explain later. Please hand me that bottle of water. This is much worse than last time. I don't know how much longer I can hold him down. I'm afraid he'll hurt himself."

"Much worse than last time?" Blue was looking even more confused.

"Quickly, the water!" shouted Pedro.

Blue rushed to the sink and snatched a bottle of drinking water. Acting quickly she splashed some water on Woodson's face. The shock seemed to work. Though not yet awake, he stopped thrashing and Pedro was able to loosen his grip. As Woodson lay there, silent and motionless, Blue gently wiped his face with a wet cloth. She spoke his name softly, hoping that he would soon regain consciousness. Woodson's eyes opened wide, body stiffened and his head began to shake back and forth.

"Whoa!" exclaimed Blue, in response to Woodson's sudden movement. "What can we do to help him?"

Woodson's eyes began to flick, glancing feverishly around the room. His body relaxed, as if he had just exhaled. He burst into tears. Sitting up, Woodson buried his face in his hands. The sobs were deep and pulsating.

"I'm okay, Blue," he said between sobs." I just had a bad dream, that's all."

"Dream! That was no dream!" scolded Blue. "If you ask me, that wouldn't even qualify as a nightmare—"

Woodson became defensive.

"It was just a bad dream. Let it go—"

Pedro got between them.

"I told her, Woody. I had to. This was much worse than the last time."

"Would you two knuckleheads tell me what's going on?" demanded Blue.

Woodson stood up and removed his sweat soaked shirt, took the water bottle from Blue, tilted his head back and emptied it.

"I have been having this horrible dream—"

"Vision, Woody," Pedro quickly corrected.

"Okay kid, a vision. You remember I told you about my dream. I see an old man and an Indian woman rowing away from the shore in a dugout canoe as the sun is beginning to set. Then, I see a mounted Spanish Conquistador in full battle dress, riding down a hill toward the beach. Then, without any warning, the canoe catches fire. I can't recall how, but I can see the man in flames—I feel the flames."

"You felt the fire again? The same as when you were a kid?" asked Blue.

"Yes, just like I did the first time. I see him engulfed in the flames. I can feel his skin on fire—I feel the horrible pain."

"Why doesn't he jump in the water?" Blue asked. Woodson gave her an impatient look. "Well, that's what I would have done" she said defensively.

"I experience the pain until I wake up," said Woodson now speaking more calmly. "I just don't know what it's all about."

"That's the same vision as Guerrero wrote about!" exclaimed Blue. "The connection between you two is undeniable. Why didn't you tell me that you were having that dream again?"

"I'm not really sure. Maybe I was afraid it would scare you. I think we'd better get packed up so that we can get started for Chichén Itzá. Maybe we can persuade Mr. Aguilar to give us some answers."

Suddenly, there was a bang on the door.

"Woody, open up. It's Lyons," called the familiar but muffled voice.

Woodson grabbed the knob and threw the door open revealing Professor Lyons.

"What are you doing here? Where's Aguilar?"

Lyons looked as if he hadn't slept in a week. His clothes were wrinkled, his tanned face was pale and his thick, gray hair appeared greasy and stuck out in all directions.

"He's leaving for Chichén Itzá, this morning. Now—I couldn't stop him!"

"I thought you two were in this thing together," said Woodson pulling Lyons inside, and looking around outside before closing the door.

"Were—is right Woody," said Lyons shaking his head.

"You've got your nerve coming here," snapped Blue.

"You're right. I lost it somehow," said Lyons holding up his hand.

"How could you betray Woody—and me?" asked Pedro.

Lyons shook his head again.

"I got myself into a little bind last year—"

"What kind of bind?" inquired Woodson.

"I lost a lot of money gambling," replied Lyons searching for the proper words." What can I say? Aguilar's offer was tempting."

"Tempting enough to put your friends in harm's way?" asked Blue. "How can we trust you?"

"You have to trust me, this guy is mad. We have to stop him."

"Why didn't you come to me?" asked Woodson. "I would have helped you."

"I know... I'm sorry." Lyons looked down at the floor and rubbed his forehead.

"Please believe me, we have to stop him," Lyons warned again.

"We know! But from what?" asked Blue.

"Look, I read some of that codex. I'm telling you, we're talking about pure evil, son," replied Lyons.

"What did you find?" asked Woodson.

Lyons sat nervously on the edge of the bed.

"That thing is like the Egyptian Book of the Dead. That fool is going to try to conjure up spirits of the ones who died in the Sacred Cenote."

"You can't really believe that, Professor," said Blue. "Woody, tell him about your vision."

"I do believe it, Blue," replied Lyons. "I read it and I'm convinced that he thinks he can do it!" Lyons paused and looked curiously at Woodson. "What vision?"

"Never mind, I'll tell you later," said Woodson as he sat next to Lyons. "What could Aguilar possibly hope to do with the codex?"

Pedro quickly interrupted.

"He believes if he can open the portal between the worlds of the living and the dead, he will become immortal and live forever."

"Does the book say that will happen?" asked Woodson.

"I don't know for sure," began Lyons, "But I think Pedro is right. That's all Aguilar spoke about after we took the codex from you yesterday."

"Believe it or not, this is starting to make sense," began Woodson. "Pedro, what about the old Aguilar's text? Can you remember anything that could help us?"

"No, Woody, but I have an idea," said Pedro.

"I'm willing to listen to just about anything at this point," he replied.

"I think that right now the only person who can help us is Gonzalo Guerrero," said Pedro grabbing the ancient cylinder and holding it out to Woodson and the others.

"That's it!" Woodson exclaimed, "We need to translate the last few pages."

"That's crazy! We need to stop Aguilar. Now!" argued Lyons.

"No, no, Pedro is right. This comes first. If we don't know exactly what Aguilar's up to, we won't be able to stop him." Woodson turned to Blue. "Blue, could you run down and bring back some food? This may take a little while."

As Blue started back to her room to get dressed, she heard Woodson call out, "Coffee, bring lots of coffee!"

We arrived in Tulum at sunset. The blinding sun reflecting off the water made it extremely difficult for the rowers to navigate the dangerous reefs that lie just off the coast. But, by the god's and the great skill of our rowers, we made it safely to shore.

I was not sure how to locate Aguilar. But, I was sure that he would know when we arrived. The city had changed so much since being taken by the Spanish. Now, the soldiers outnumbered the Maya. As we walked along the path to the square and El Castillo, we were subjected to many insults and threats made in my native tongue. Because of my sun darkened skin and native tattoos, the soldiers did not recognize me as a Spaniard and did not tell that I understood their slurs and insults.

Once we arrived at El Castillo, we were met by a Mayan priest who directed us to a small building at the base of the temple that the Spanish clergy were using as their headquarters. The priest entered before us and lit several torches to light our way. Even by the light of a single torch I could see the damage done by the Spaniards. Crosses, and religious images of Christianity, were painted everywhere. All the Mayan art had been removed. Without even thinking, I fell to my knees and made the sign of the cross. My God, I could not remember the last time.

Then, as I knelt there, I felt the presence of another as he entered the room. My wife reached for me as I got to my feet and held me tightly. I could hear a voice behind me. When I turned, I was face to face with the monster—Aguilar. He motioned me outside, asking that Zazhal ab remain. He assured me that no harm would come to her.

Once outside, we sat by a fire. Aguilar offered some refreshment but I declined.

Very few words were spoken. After what seemed like a very long time, he looked at me and asked with no emotion where the codex was hidden. I told him that it was somewhere safe and that the evil in the codex must be hidden forever. His stare burned through my very soul. Aguilar ranted and raved about how I did not, or could not; understand the power of the codex.

I questioned Aguilar of this power that he spoke of. All that he told me was that it possessed the power to give man eternal life. Aguilar went on to explain many things that I already knew... except for one, he had mistakenly told Bishop de Landa about the codex and now the Church wanted to know more. It seemed that Aguilar was able to persuade the priest that I had entrusted with the codex, to help him translate it before I took it back many years before.

Then his mood changed. I could feel the evil and the frustration grow within him. Over and over again he threatened us with death if we did not reveal where it was. I would not tell him. I would die first!

Some time later, Zazhal ab and I were led to a small building and held under guard. From this building I am now making my last entry into this journal. Then, I know I must hide it here. For soon I fear the soldiers will take us from here to kill us. Aguilar must not find what I have written about the codex.

In the morning, just before sunrise, I awoke to a commotion outside the tiny building. Then, suddenly the Mayan priest, whom we met the night before, entered. Silently he placed a large wooden tray with tortillas and cups of warm mush on the small alter that was centered in the room. Beneath the food was a large sheet of writing material. The priest motioned us to eat. Then under his breath he said that they would be coming for us soon. Then, motioning to the writing material on the tray, he indicated that I should read. Finally, he backed slowly out through the doorway.

Carefully, I pulled the paper from underneath the food and turned it over. Neither, Zazhal ab or I could understand what the glyphs of Mayan writing meant. I hope that whoever finds my journals *can translate them. I also hope that the vessel that I have carried them in will stand the test of time. For it must be of great importance. Aguilar will be coming soon and I know not what will become of us. To you, who will find this journal, may the gods smile on your life as they have on my own.*

Gonzalo Guerrero
As translated by R. Woodson

Woodson sat back to collect his thoughts, before taking on this new challenge. The room was quiet. His thoughts were of Guerrero and his wife and what became of them. Guerrero's translations were complete and all that remained was the mysterious sheet that was given to him by the Mayan holy man just before he hid the cylinder. Woodson finally sat up and spread the ancient paper out onto a table. After a few minutes of intense study, he sat back and admitted with a shrug.

"I don't have a clue," he said looking around the room. "Pedro? Blue? Lyons? Anybody got any ideas?"

"I think I might know what this means Woody," said Pedro as he pointed at one of the glyphs on the mysterious sheet. "But I need to speak to Angel."

"What is it, Kid?" asked Woodson.

"I think it might be a way to stop Aguilar," said Pedro

"How so?" asked Lyons.

"Do you see this figure here?" Pedro asked, again pointing at the first glyph on the page.

"Yes, its looks like an old, toothless man with a very large nose. Possibly God L." replied Blue.

"That is God L! The god who ruled the Underworld, I'm sure of it," said Pedro. The others could hear the excitement in his voice as he continued. "God L presided over the assembly of Gods when the cosmos was ordered in the Mayan date of 4 Ahau 8 Cunku—the Maya beginning of time."

"Yes, Pedro, that could be it." Woodson paused. "Now, if I can remember from my old college days—God L ruled, Xibalba, the Underworld, and from the beginning of time, Maya time, he would guide chosen ones back from the Underworld..."

Lyons quickly finished Woodson's thought.

"...Back from the dead, into the light of life. That's it! Why didn't I see that? Geez, I used to teach this stuff."

"Now look at this symbol," continued Pedro, "It must represent the Sacred Cenote at Chichén Itzá."

"So, we were right! Aguilar is going to the Cenote," said Woodson. "You're smarter than you look, Kid. Where'd you learn all this? Never mind I know, Angel."

Pedro nodded, a toothy smile spread across his dark,

young face.

Woodson stared at the symbols again, his face betrayed his puzzlement.

"There's just one thing. How will Aguilar do it?" he asked. "How can he pass into the underworld and back again?"

"I don't know, Woody," began Pedro, "That's why I thought of calling Angel. He's a shaman, he knows the ancient ways."

Blue pointed to another glyph; the one centered in the page.

"I know that glyphs aren't my expertise, but isn't this the one about sacrifice in the Sacred Cenote?" she inquired.

"Yeah, I think it is," said Woodson as he bent over the table again. 'What about it?"

"Maybe Aguilar needs to sacrifice a human being to make this whole thing work." Her voice trailed off as the shocking words left her lips.

"What did you say?" asked Woodson staring at Blue in disbelief.

"I said—"

"I heard you—Pedro, call Angel."

CHAPTER EIGHTEEN

Kidnapped

"When does Angel arrive?" asked Woodson as he and Pedro checked into their room at the Mayaland Hotel in Chichén Itzá.

"He should be here any time. He was going to clear his schedule and take the next flight out, said he wouldn't miss this for the world."

Blue entered the room without knocking.

"Anybody hungry?" she asked.

"Are you always hungry Blue?" snapped Woodson. "We just ate before leaving Cozumel an hour ago."

"Hey, take it easy," she snapped, "I just asked. Look, I'm going to get an ice cream bar. I'll be in the lobby. See ya."

"Don't wander off. We're heading out as soon as Angel gets here. Got it?"

"Sure, sure, don't worry." Blue started for the door.

"Oh Blue," Woodson called out after her, "If you should see Lyons, tell him to stop by."

"Okay." she said as she left the room, closing the door behind her.

"She sure eats a lot, doesn't she," commented

Pedro.

Woodson smiled and nodded his head. No words were needed. Minutes later, there was a knock on the door. Professor Lyons walked in, eating an ice cream bar.

"Oh good, it's you," said Woodson, "You must have run into Blue in the lobby."

"Nope, I didn't see her at all," Lyons replied between slurps.

"She was going down for ice cream. I told her that if she saw you to ask you to come see me."

"Nope... didn't see her."

"You must have just missed her. C'mon in and sit down, there are some things that we need to go over before Angel arrives."

Blue stood in line waiting to pay for her ice cream, when an older man with a bushy gray moustache, dressed all in white, dark glasses and a straw hat waddled up to her. The man asked Blue if she could direct him to the entrance to the ruins. Blue politely asked him to wait until she paid for her ice cream and the man agreed. Assuming he was a tourist, Blue took the old gentleman by the arm, walked him out the main entrance to the hotel, and pointed him in the direction of the gate.

"Just follow all those folks with the cameras. You can't miss it," she said politely.

The old man peeked toward the gate over his dark glasses and turned to Blue.

"Could you please walk with me?" he inquired timidly. "I am afraid I will surely get lost."

"Look mister, just follow the crowd. Okay?" replied Blue, quickly becoming impatient.

"No, I must insist that you walk with me miss," said the man, his voice beginning to roughen.

"Look, I don't have—" Blue suddenly felt the muzzle of a gun press sharply into her side. "—on second thought, maybe I should walk with you."

"Okay guys, listen up," began Woodson, trying to get everyone's attention. Angel had arrived a few moments earlier and was engaged in an animated discussion with Pedro and Lyons. "Let's get to work, okay?"

"Aguilar can't do a thing until the park closes at sunset," said Lyons, "I've arranged for us to go in undisturbed, but I'm sure he has as well."

"You're on, my friend," said Woodson turning to Angel. "What happens when we get in there? Do we head straight for the Sacred Cenote?"

"Pedro and I will head for the Platform of Venus," began Angel, "Near the sacbé leading to the cenote. That has to be our base. Nothing can get in or out of the cenote area without going by it. Lyons and Blue will—"

"Where is Blue?" interrupted Woodson, "she should have been back a while ago."

"Maybe we should go look for her, Woody," said Pedro.

"We probably should, though I would bet she's in the restaurant with her hands wrapped around a big old, juicy, cheeseburger. We'll plan this after we find her. We still have an hour before sunset."

"Who are you—and what do you want with me?" demanded Blue, as her captor led her to a small, secluded clearing in the jungle just behind the Temple of the Warriors. The stranger still held the gun pressed uncomfortably against her side; when he suddenly bent down and picked something up from the ground.

"Maybe you will recognize this, my pretty friend." The stranger held what looked like a package wrapped in old leather.

"Aguilar!" she exclaimed, recognizing the codex.

"At your service," he said, removing his disguise, revealing a round pink face with a bulbous nose and a pair of deep-set, sinister looking black eyes.

"What do you want with me?" she gasped, finally seeing Aguilar's real face.

"You'll find out soon enough, my pretty," said Aguilar, as he shot Blue a threatening smile. "Suffice it to say that you will soon be making the supreme sacrifice."

Aguilar's chilling tone sent shivers down Blue's spine.

"She's nowhere to be found, Woody. If she is in this hotel I couldn't tell you where," said Lyons.

"How about the ladies room?" asked Pedro.

"I checked them all," answered Woodson.

"So, that's what all that screaming was about," chided Pedro.

"Seriously, Woody, where could she be?" asked Lyons.

A small, round, gray haired woman marched up to, Woodson, and slapped him right across the face.

"Ouch!" he exclaimed quickly grabbing his cheek.

"Friend of yours?" laughed Pedro.

"An old friend from the ladies room," Woodson said, still rubbing his cheek. "Look, it's possible that she just wandered off and lost track of time. She loves ruins—she could be anywhere."

"I hope she doesn't run into Aguilar," said Pedro.

"He's right, Woody," said Lyons. "He's got to be here—somewhere."

"It's possible, but I still think she's somewhere with her hands wrapped around a cheeseburger," said Woodson.

Lyons shuddered, his face suddenly paled.

"Pedro, you did say that there is a possibility that Aguilar was going to have to perform some type of sacrifice?" he asked.

"I did," began Pedro, "But I figured that it would be symbolic, you know, maybe a chicken. I'm sure he wouldn't—"

"Look, he was acting real strange when I left him. I told you guys that he was losing it," said Lyons. "Believe me, I think this guy is capable of resorting to something horrible."

"Okay then—we need to go to plan B," said Woodson, slapping an open palm with his fist.

"Plan B?" asked Angel.

"He means we're going to have to make it up as we go along," said Pedro.

"Right! Now let's find Blue!" exclaimed Woodson.

"What are you planning to do with me?" asked Blue. Aguilar had placed her on the ground, hands bound tightly behind her back.

"You will learn soon enough... at sunset to be precise," replied Aguilar.

"Woody and the guys are probably looking for me right now," she warned.

"I'm sure they are, but it will be too late." Aguilar looked up at the sky, rubbed his hands together and helped Blue up to her feet.

"Time to go, Ms. Blue, the Underworld is calling." Aguilar cackled loudly. Blue shivered at the sound of his mad laughter.

"What does that mean?"

"You'll find out soon enough, young lady. Now, get moving."

"We need to head directly to the cenote Woody. Aguilar may have already taken her there," gasped Angel, losing his breath trying to keep up with Woodson, who was now running toward the entrance to the ruins.

"I hope we're not too late, Angel," said Woodson looking back at his old friend.

"Remember," said the shaman still gasping for breath, "He can do nothing until sunset when all of the tourists are gone."

Pedro appeared just as Woodson and Angel approached the gate. A thick coil of rope draped neatly over his shoulder.

"Angel," he shouted, "Here's the rope you wanted."

"What on earth is that for?" asked Woodson.

"Trust me on this," he sighed, grateful that he could finally stop a moment and catch his breath. Angel was breathing very hard and looked as if he were about to faint.

"You okay, Grandfather?" Pedro noticed that Angel was having trouble catching his breath. The young man had never really been aware of his grandfather's age until that moment. To him, Angel had always been... Angel: strong and vibrant and forever young, but now—

Angel could see the concern in grandson's eyes. A

wide grin spread across the old man's face.

"Si, Little One... Angel will be fine."

Pedro looked relieved. With his parents gone, Angel and his grandmother were all the family he had. For the first time that he could remember, Pedro didn't mind Angel calling him Little One.

Lyons met them at the entrance after he secured entry to the park.

"We must hurry. The sun is setting quickly," said Angel, still fighting for breath.

Woodson led the way as they entered the ancient city of Chichén Itzá that by this time had been emptied of tourists. Quickly they headed down a back road reserved for maintenance and restoration traffic. Before they had gotten very far, the two goons that were with Aguilar and Lyons at San Gervasio, stepped out of the brush, waving their pistols.

Woodson stretched his arms out to his sides and quickly stopped his friends.

"They don't look like they're here to talk," he said softly over his shoulder. "Let me handle this—follow my lead." Woodson motioned for his friends to stay back as he walked toward the gun waving goons. "I had a feeling I'd run into you two. Look, we don't have time for this, boys—put your guns away before someone gets hurt."

"Don't move," said the goon with the gold teeth, "We've got all the time in the world. So just sit tight until we get the word from Aguilar."

"Look you two—you have no idea what this is all about. We're talking murder one, boys. If Aguilar succeeds in killing Blue, you boys are going to swing."

The two men glanced at each other. The one with the gold teeth shook his head and shrugged.

"That's right boys," Woodson continued, "They still hang a man for murder in Mexico. Right Pedro?"

"Uh—" Pedro quickly covered his surprise. "That's right," he said, trying not to smile, "Had an uncle once, the old guy stole a horse. They—uh—strung him up right after the trial."

The goons again shot each other an uneasy glance.

Pedro continued his narrative.

"Yeah, they took him right out into the square and—"

"Thank you, Pedro," said Woodson," I think they get the idea—"

"It was ugly, really ugly." Pedro was on a roll. "The way he danced—" Angel slapped Pedro in the back of the head. "What was that for?" he asked.

"I think they got the message," whispered Angel through clenched teeth.

Woodson looked back at Pedro, to make sure he was done with his interesting narrative. Turning back toward the goons he said, "If I were you two, I'd give this a lot of thought," he said.

The men stepped closer together, whispering back and forth. As their conversation grew more animated, Woodson saw his chance, without another word, he leaped toward them. So quickly had he caught them off guard, that they were both knocked to the ground before they could fire a shot. Without thinking, Pedro rushed to Woodson's aid, kicking the gun from one of the thug's hands. Meanwhile, Woodson struggled with the other gunman.

"Angel. Stop Aguilar!" he yelled as both men fought for the gun. "Find Blue!"

CHAPTER NINETEEN

The Truth

"What are we doing here?" cried Blue, as Aguilar led her to the edge of the Sacred Cenote.

"I believe we are going to perform a sacrifice, my dear," said Aguilar, his face contorted with a wicked smile, "Yours!"

"You're crazy. You can't be serious about throwing me into that well," snapped Blue.

"It's necessary to complete my plan to become as one with the Underworld," replied Aguilar.

Blue's heart sank as she looked down into the cenote's murky water sixty feet below. She knew that if the fall didn't kill her, she would surely drown in the deep water. The Sacred Cenote at Chichén Itzá was an ancient sinkhole. The underground river systems that run throughout the Yucatan Peninsula will occasionally cause weakened areas of limestone to collapse into the water table below leaving a large, round, deep, rocky well. These cenote's are the Yucatan's main source of fresh water. Blue thought of how the ancient Mayan believed the cenote at Chichén Itzá to be sacred; a portal to the underworld for sacrificial victims.

Blue's thoughts were suddenly broken when Aguilar started reading from the codex. When she turned to look behind, there stood Aguilar holding the codex up above his head gesturing wildly to the gods.

My god, she thought, Where were the security people? Why weren't the clean up crews making their rounds? Where was Woody? Unexpectedly there came an echoing shout from down the rocky causeway that lead to the cenote.

"Stop, Aguilar! Stop now!" It was Angel with Lyons and they were running toward them. Angel waved his arms wildly over his head. "You do not understand the power you are about to release!"

Aguilar ignored the warning and continued to chant in ancient Maya, all the time pushing Blue ever closer to the edge of the well. The sound of a gunshot filled the air. Angel and Lyons quickly stopped and turned around to see where it came from.

"Woody!" cried Blue, as she strained furiously against her bonds. She felt the thin ropes that bound her wrists begin to loosen.

Aguilar stopped chanting and turned viciously on Angel.

"No, my little friend, it is you who must stop or this pretty little lady here will meet her end—much sooner than expected."

"Let her go!" yelled Lyons. "Don't be a fool. You can't get away with this."

The sound of a second gunshot filled the air. Aguilar's eyes widened, the edges of his mouth curled up.

"By the sound of those gunshots—it would seem that I already have," growled Aguilar, inching Blue even closer to her impending doom.

"If you do this, you will unleash powers that you could not possibly understand," pleaded Angel. "Stop now and there might still be a chance for you."

"Oh, but I do know the powers that I am about to unleash, my little man. Know—that when I finish the incantation, it will summon the power of God L and the portal of Sak-Bak-Nakan. When I throw this lovely young lady over the edge, the Serpent Bar will open the portal to the Underworld. According to this codex, I will become immortal!" exclaimed Aguilar. His voice cracked with an insane excitement. Then, just as he was about to complete the vile ceremony, a shadowy figure burst from the jungle.

"Not so fast, Aguilar, your little party is about to come to an end!"

"Woody!" screamed Blue. "You're alive!"

"You bet I am, Blue," yelled Woodson. "Now, let her go!"

Aguilar pushed Blue closer to the edge.

"One more step, Mr. Woodson and your girlfriend here is in the cenote."

"This won't work, Aguilar. These are myths. You

cannot become immortal," explained Woodson.

Angel quickly got Woodson's attention and mouthed one word. Pedro?

Woodson could see the anguished look of concern on his old friends face. With a reassuring wink of his eye, Woodson could see Angels look of concern instantly vanish.

"Oh, but I will," replied Aguilar. "And you will be helpless to do anything but watch."

"Why?" inquired Woodson, attempting to distract Aguilar.

"My ancestor spent many years trying to posses this codex," began Aguilar, "He knew with it, true immortality could be achieved. He failed—I will not."

"Why do you think you will succeed?" Woodson was still buying time until he could figure his next move.

"Just before Guerrero stole the codex, Aguilar had learned its secrets and was ready to make the journey to the Underworld and immortality."

"Then, Aguilar did not intend to burn the codex as Guerrero saw in his vision?"

"No, he would pretend to burn it and deceive Bishop de Landa."

"Of course," interrupted Angel, "Aguilar would have been ex-communicated from the church. Possibly put to death. He needed to fool the church into thinking he destroyed the codex."

"Exactly!" exclaimed the smiling Aguilar. "Now, if

you gentlemen will excuse, me I have a new world to meet."

Woodson took one step closer, causing Aguilar to stiffen.

"Did Aguilar kill Guerrero?" Woodson asked hastily.

"What?" Aguilar asked, his tone incredulous.

"You've read your ancestor's journal. Did he finally get his revenge?" pressed Woodson.

"Yes... he did," said Aguilar proudly.

"How?"

"It seems that while they were holding Guerrero and his wife, Aguilar pleaded with de Landa to allow him to torture Guerrero until he told where the codex was hidden. By this time, the Bishop had softened his approach in dealing with the Maya and had regretted the burning and destruction of their history. He commanded Aguilar to release Guerrero and to never pursue the codex again."

"What did Aguilar do then?" asked Woodson.

"He commanded his men to soak Guerrero's dugout canoe with oil and then when—"

Woodson stopped him in mid sentence. "—then he had his archers fire flaming arrows at them when they were offshore—"

Aguilar finished, "—the canoe burst into flames, setting them both on fire and eventually sinking it and their bodies, leaving no trace and no investigation by Bishop de Landa. Very clever, wouldn't you say?"

Woodson stumbled backwards, dizzy and disoriented, he grabbed his head. It was then that Blue saw the small red patch on his shoulder.

"Woody, you're hurt!" she cried out, as she felt the tears well up in her eyes.

Woodson shook his head. "It's nothing, Blue, just a scratch."

"Then, what's wrong?" she asked.

"Remember my vision? That was it. I could see and feel it as it happened."

Aguilar's eyes opened wide as if he had been struck by lightening.

"Then it will work. Don't you see? The spirits are reaching out! You have been touched by Guerrero's spirit, just as the spirit of my ancestor has indeed touched me. Now, if you will excuse me gentlemen, I will attempt to wake some even older spirits."

Aguilar read from the codex again, the sun was setting fast and he knew the time had come. A wind was howling, swirling all around the Sacred Cenote. As the wind intensified, Aguilar shouted out the ancient Mayan prayers—dangerous prayers that had not been uttered for centuries.

The water from the center of the well started to rise. Formed in the shape of a thundering waterspout, it reached far above the spot where Aguilar and Blue stood, the water spray swirled in circles over their heads. The noise from the wind became deafening, as if hundreds of Mayan spirits signaled the coming of evil, by blowing through conch shells all at one time.

"Stop," cried Angel, trying to be heard above the roar "You will not be able to control God L. No one in this or the other world can control him. He is master in the world of the dead."

From the top of the waterspout, came a cloud of vapor. Slowly it began to take shape. As the vapor swirled and struggled to fight the winds a form appeared from the mist. First, long sinewy arms extended from the waterspout, then a head. Aguilar was now screaming out the incantations, his face the color of rage, he had become a man possessed. Blue continued to struggle against the ropes forcing them to loosen even more.

As the vaporous form solidified, there appeared the face of a toothless old man. The form had a large nose that squared off at the very end. Woodson recognized it immediately. It was God L. Master of the Underworld. From the mist, longing, hideous hands reached for Blue. Woodson saw Aguilar's free arm move toward Blue's back. There was no doubt of what Aguilar was about to do.

With a quick shove Blue was literally teetering on the edge of the cenote. She barely felt the push that sent her, head first, into the cenote. At that same instant Blue felt the ropes fall from her wrists. She was free. But was it too late? As she fell, head first into the cenote, Blue grabbed wildly for anything that might stop her fall. Somehow her hands found the branch of a short bush that grew straight out of the gray limestone wall just below the cenote rim.

Blue screamed as she dangled over the murky water. She knew that the only thing that stood between life and certain death was the strength of the branch that she now perilously hung from.

Woodson leaped for the edge of the cenote straining to reach Blue. Blue's weight was proving to be too much for the tiny branch; She began to slide farther down the now bent bush inches farther from Woodson's outstretched hand. Woodson felt the desperate kicks to his side as Aguilar attempted to stop him from saving Blue.

Rapidly, another dark figure burst from the jungle. It was Pedro, still carrying Angel's rope. Before Aguilar could react, Pedro rushed to the edge of the cenote and pushed him away from Woodson.

Angel lunged toward Aguilar and grabbed for the codex, but Aguilar was just tall enough to keep it from shaman's reach. The wind became stronger and the roar grew so deafening that even Blue's screams could no longer be heard. Angel knew the gods had been angered. He chanted to the gods while struggling for the codex. One way or another, he had to stop the growing madness. The wind grew stronger pulling the codex from Aguilar's sweaty grip and into the hands of the misty outstretched arms of God L. The codex danced above the water as the vaporous hands caressed it. Angel and Aguilar stared at the misty vision in disbelief.

"Noooo!" Aguilar's screams were the screams of a desperate man.

Pedro threw the end of the rope over the edge. "Grab the rope!" he cried.

"I can't," was Blue's frantic reply. "I can't... I'll fall!" Blue's arms were beginning to fatigue, the spiny branch burned through her tight grip. The wet swirling wind conspired to bring her closer to death, but Blue grasped the wet branch with all her strength, refusing to give up.

Woodson jumped to his feet and tied the end of the rope around his waist.

"I'm going down there, Pedro," screamed Woodson trying to be heard over the howling winds. "You and Lyons will have to lower me down—I'll signal for you to pull us up." Pedro and Lyons both nodded.

"But Woody," cried Pedro, "the rope is getting wet. I don't know if I am strong enough to—"

"You'll be fine, Pedro." Then pointing toward the cenote Lyons said, "You better get going, Woody, or we'll lose Blue."

Woodson checked the loop around his waist.

"Okay—hold on tight!" he exclaimed before disappearing over the edge.

Woodson's weight pulled Pedro toward the edge, Lyons, who had grabbed the rope behind him struggled with the weight as well.

"I'm afraid I'm not much help, Pedro," cried the professor, while struggling to keep his footing on the wet limestone.

"Just hold on, Professor!" exclaimed Pedro.

Woodson had now scrambled across the wet limestone wall to Blue, she was soaking wet and even in the diminishing light Woodson could see the look of terror on her face.

"What took you so long?" she asked sarcastically. Blue's confidence had been restored with Woodson's arrival. "Do you think I've got nothing better to do then hang around here all day waiting for you," she cried.

Woodson shook his head and grabbed Blue firmly around the waist.

"Grab me around the neck and pull yourself around so we're face to face and wrap your legs around my waist."

Blue turned and grabbed Woodson around the neck. The mist from God L pelted their faces and soaked their clothes, but Blue managed to get into position. Woodson smiled, "We're in this together, Blue!" he exclaimed over the roaring water. "Hold on!" Woodson looked up toward the rim of the cenote and shouted as loud as he could. "Now!"

Pedro felt his feet slip as he attempted to steady

himself on the soaked limestone. He and Lyons struggled even more with Blue's added weight. They were slowly being pulled toward the edge of the cenote.

Woodson looked helplessly at Blue as they slowly descended toward the agitated waters below.

Angel looked away from Aguilar to see his grandson and Professor Lyons moving closer toward the edge. Without thinking he reached back and punched Aguilar squarely on the jaw. The impact sent Aguilar reeling. Angel rushed to help pull Woodson and Blue to safety. Nearly reaching the rope Angel felt a pair of hands grab him from behind and pull him to the ground. It was Aguilar. Holding Angel down, he began laughing like as if he were mad, watching Pedro and Lyons inch ever closer to the edge of the cenote.

Pedro strained against the rope with all his might, his arms ached and hands burned raw against the slippery rope.

"Pull Professor! Pull harder!" he screamed but still the weight pulled him closer to the edge.

"It's no use," cried the professor, "We can't hold them much longer!"

Angel screamed and kicked wildly at Aguilar to release him but the old man was no match for the younger Aguilar.

"I won't let them die," screamed Pedro. He strained mightily but the toe of his front foot was now at the very edge. Suddenly, the load felt lighter, Pedro was now moving back, away from the cenote's edge. Did someone come to help them, he thought. He looked back but no one had joined the struggle. Yet, they were moving back. How?

Further and further they pulled away from the edge, the weight felt lighter with every step. Aguilar began to curse. Angel stared in disbelief. Pedro looked back at Lyons; the professor wore a surprised look, but still pulled with all his might.

Pedro blinked his eyes. There was now something behind the professor, a shape. Pedro wasn't sure, but it looked as if it was pulling the rope. Someone was helping them. Pedro could barely make them out through the mist. It was a woman. A Mayan woman, but where did she come from?

Pedro's strength was renewed, the young apprentice dug in with all his might and pulled. First, Woodson's hat appeared, then his face then Blue's back. They were so close—he pulled again as hard as he could. Woodson grabbed the edge of the cenote and hoisted Blue to safety. Pedro gave one last all out effort and Woodson joined her at the top. .

The winds began to intensify; the sky was becoming night and the howling of the cenote even more deafening. Pedro dropped the rope and pulled Aguilar off of Angel.

While the winds continued to howl around the misty image of God L, the codex danced over its giant fingertips, as if it meant to tease and taunt Aguilar. Woodson pulled himself up and backed away from the edge of the cenote. Pedro and Lyons rushed to his side.

"Get back," yelled Woodson as he let the rope drop from his waist.

God L was now as one with the wind that swirled around the sacred cenote. The face, the arms, the hands all became a misty blur, the codex was no longer visible—vanished—swallowed by the watery God L. Suddenly the waterspout collapsed, as if sucked into a vacuum, back into the cenote, taking the codex and God L beneath the murky depths forever. The winds quickly ceased, silence descended on the cenote.

Aguilar pushed Pedro away and peered over the edge.

"No, no, it can't be. I must have that book!" he cried breaking the silence. Aguilar made a move as if he were to jump into the cenote.

"Oh no, you don't!" cried Angel, as he reached out and grabbed Aguilar by the collar. "It's over, Aguilar. Let it go!"

Pedro joined Lyons, Blue and Woodson at the cenote's edge.

"When I heard those shots, I thought you were dead, for sure," Blue cried.

"So did I," gasped Woodson. "I guess we're all going to be okay, except maybe for him." Woodson pointed at Aguilar, who now lay face down at the very edge of the cenote wall, still held in Angel's firm grip, and still crying out to the spirits.

"What just happened here, Angel?" asked Woodson.

"My guess is that God L didn't want Blue or Aguilar in his world. It seems that all he wanted was the codex," replied Angel.

"If it wasn't for that woman who helped us—" began Pedro, as he placed his hand on Woodson's shoulder.

Lyons gave Pedro a puzzled look.

"What woman?" he asked.

The one that grabbed the rope behind you," said Pedro. "Where is she?"

Angel looking quizzically at Pedro and said, "I saw no one,"

Pedro looked confused.

"Wait a minute... I'm sure—"

"There was no one," replied Angel.

Pedro looked scared.

"I'm sure I saw a Mayan woman," he said, his voice trembling. "She grabbed the rope and pulled—I saw—I swear!"

"Blue and I were a little busy," said Woodson. "We didn't see anything. What is Pedro talking about?"

"You are sure, that is what you saw?" asked Angel.

Pedro took a deep breath and pointed toward the spot where he had last seen the woman.

"She was there, I tell you!" he exclaimed.

"Another spirit perhaps," said Woodson turning to Angel. "There have been some really strange things happening since we found that cylinder, Angel," continued Woodson, as he threw the rope to Pedro. "What about all that spirit stuff Aguilar was talking about? You know—about my connection to Guerrero."

"You know, Woody," interrupted Pedro, as he tied Aguilar's hands, "Maybe Guerrero all along has guided you. I think that what you have experienced was your fate—the spirit of Guerrero was your guide."

"Is he right?" Woodson asked Angel.

"My grandson has learned well," replied Angel. "I think his explanation is possible."

"Could I be Guerrero reincarnated?"

"Maybe you are," said Angel," Only the Gods know for sure. There is a reason and purpose for everything, Woody. But know this... somewhere deep inside is the knowledge of what took place many years ago. You have been chosen, somehow to see what no one else could. In doing so, you and Pedro, were successful in keeping the two worlds apart."

"But who was that woman? And how come I was the only one who could see her?" asked Pedro.

Angel held a finger gently to his lips.

"Shhh, Little One. We may never know. All we can do is be grateful for her help. Without her our friends might have died."

"Do you think Woody will still have those horrible

dreams, Angel?" asked Pedro.

"I think not," began Angel," But do not be surprised if there are not other dreams and visions. You have been touched Woody—you as well, Little One. Embrace it!"

A security guard approached the cenote holding his gun on Aguilar's men.

"Here's another one you can hand over to the police," said Pedro. The guard pulled Aguilar to his feet and led all three men away.

"I told you that rope would come in handy," said Angel through a toothy smile.

Woodson shook his head and replied, "I'll never doubt you again my old friend."

"Now what, Woody?" asked Blue, her arms still held tightly around Woodson's neck.

"First of all, we're going to hand both Guerrero's and the old Aguilar's journals over to Lyons. They belong in a museum. Then I guess Pedro and I should head back to Tulum to finish the restoration."

"Going back to work sounds great," laughed Pedro. "I could use the rest."

"Mind if I tag along, Woody?" asked Blue, arms still hugging him tightly.

"I was counting on it," he replied.

Later that night, Woodson had just sat back in his room, at the Mayaworld Hotel, recovering from the experience at the cenote, when he heard a knock on the door. It was Lyons, he had stopped by to say goodbye before leaving for Mexico City.

"Heading out tonight Woody. I just wanted to apologize again for all of the trouble I caused." Lyons pointed at Woodson's shoulder. "How's that wound doing, amigo?"

"It's nothing." Woodson glanced at the white dressing on his bare shoulder. "I know you thought that you were doing the best thing for yourself," he said, looking up. "You just didn't realize what you were getting into."

"I sold out—I betrayed—you—my friends for money," Lyons replied sadly.

"Its okay, Professor. I've forgiven Pedro; I think I can forgive you."

"Thanks Woody. I'll never forget this little adventure."

Woodson nodded in silent agreement.

"Do you have the two cylinders and all of the writings?"

"Absolutely!" said Lyons as he gave his leather knapsack a gentle pat. "I'll see you Woody, take care of yourself."

"What about that little gambling problem?" asked Woodson. "You should have come to me, Professor, I would have helped. I still will."

"I know," said Lyons softly. "I can tell you this - it

will never happen again."

Lyons held out his hand and the two friends shook. As Woodson pulled away, he felt something in his hand; Lyons had passed him the green beads that had been found in Guerrero's cylinder.

Woodson gave the professor a puzzled look.

"What about these?"

"Keep them Woody," said Lyons. "You deserve them. Besides, no one will ever know—except you and me," Lyons stepped through the open doorway and stopped. "What about you and Blue? Think it will work this time?"

"You know, Professor, it just might."

"Where is she by the way? I wanted to say goodbye to her and Pedro."

"Probably down in the dining room. You know Blue—always hungry."

Woodson stared down at Guerrero's beads for some minutes after Lyons had left. His thoughts disturbed by the sound of the door opening, he looked up to see Pedro entering the room. Woodson tossed the beads carelessly onto the bed.

"Did Lyons find you before he left?" asked Woodson.

Pedro nodded.

"Blue and Angel too," he replied.

"Are you okay with the professor?" asked Woodson.

"I think so," Pedro said thoughtfully. "I just don't get why he did it. I'm just a kid, Woody. This stuff is really hard to understand, I never thought that Lyons, of all people, would betray us."

Woodson's hand found his young friends shoulder.

"Money often makes people behave...differently. Your grandfather can help you understand that better than I ever could."

Pedro nodded again, the adventure made him understand how important relationships and the trust that goes with them truly were.

Woodson picked the beads up from the bed and handed them to his assistant.

"There is one thing I can tell you Pedro, we will never forget Gonzalo Guerrero or The Fifth Codex!"

THE END

Preview

Site Q: The Lost City

The Call

The old man had awakened suddenly. Was it a dream? He glanced at the window to see the light of the full moon as it poured into his small but tidy hut. He slept on the floor just as his ancestors had for over a thousand years. Was it a vision? His mind turned back to the strange images that came to disturb his rest.

The years had been kind to him, he thought as he sat up. The old man thanked the gods that at his age he could still move around without pain or effort. Now fully awake, he moved from his mat and stood. Again, the old man thanked the gods. Picking up a long stick, he poked at the smoldering wood in his fire pot. It took a few minutes, but the embers began to glow. Soon the old man would feel the gentle warmth of his fire as it covered his wrinkled face and hands.

Pulling on his coat he walked outside to fetch wood for the hungry fire. As he stood before his hut, the moon bathed him in a shimmering pale blue light. It was very bright on this night. He stopped and just stared at the mysterious disc that hung so gently in the sky. He wondered what his ancestors felt, a thousand years before, when they viewed this miracle in the sky. The old man stared up into the heavens. It was difficult to resist thinking that what had awakened him on this night was more than a dream. He had no doubt that there was a reason for this vision. He thought of how odd it was. The woman, the island, what did it all mean?

He decided it best to sit down in the night air and let the light of the moon guide his varied thoughts. Remembering this vision was not a problem. Now deeply etched in his memory, it was very real; much too real. What could it mean? He decided to replay the images in his mind. Over and over he thought about the vision, but found no answer. One thing he did know was that some day, he would meet the one. The one who would help him understand what had invaded his thoughts. The thoughts that would, undoubtedly, haunt him until he met the one.

The summer was hot; about as hot as Woodson could ever remember. He had spent so many years in the Yucatan Peninsula that he had forgotten how darn hot Chicago summers could get. His face was narrow with strong deep features that ended at a handsome square jaw. A well-known archeologist, Richard Woodson was an expert in ancient Mayan culture, including the mysterious ruins that the Maya had left behind. Woodson sat on the patio looking out over the still, mirror like lake. He thought of how he longed to return to Mexico. He missed Pedro and Angel and the wonderful sights and smells of the Caribbean.

Woodson was currently on a leave of absence

from his archeological duties. The University thought it best that he rested after his ordeal at Chichén Itzá. So he and his girlfriend, Marilynn Trotter (whom he called Blue because of her brilliant blue eyes), were back in the Windy City for some rest and relaxation.

"Hey Woody," said Blue from just inside the patio door carrying two tall, frosty glasses. "Could you get the door? My hands are full." Woodson jumped up to assist her. As he did, he accidentally dropped a string of small, green beads.

"Are you still playing with those silly beads?" Blue asked.

"I guess so," he answered, looking into her big blue eyes. "I just can't get Guerrero out of my mind."

"Look, Lyons told me to keep an eye on you. I know what an emotional roller coaster you were on last month, but you've got to let it go!" Blue sat down next to Woodson and placed her hand affectionately on his. He looked at the beads in his hand and then deeply into her eyes.

"I wish I could," he said softly, "but I miss Pedro, Angel and the professor. My God, if it weren't for them and the mysterious woman that Pedro said helped pull us to safety, the Sacred Cenote would have swallowed us up."

"I know," said Blue thoughtfully. "But that whole mess is over and done with. The Fifth Codex is lost forever and all you have left are those green beads that you found with Guerrero's journal." Blue grew impatient. "Need I remind you that you're supposed to be resting?"

Woodson stood and walked near the grassy shore. The lake appeared as smooth as glass, rare for a usually windy time of year. Standing at the water's edge for a moment, he paused, looked at the beads and then quickly stuffed them in his pocket before turning around.

"You're right. You're absolutely right," he agreed. "The Codex is gone. Guerrero's journal is in the Museum and Aguilar is in jail—" He heard the phone ring from inside.

"I'll get it," shouted Blue as she ran into the house. Moments later, she stepped back outside with the phone. "It's for you."

"Who is it?" he asked.

"He said his name was Jon Panzer. Said that it's really important that he speak with you," Blue frowned as she handed him the phone. "Do you know him?"

Woodson shrugged his shoulders and snatched the phone from Blue. "This is Woodson... yes... I'm the one... University? No... yes I can... tomorrow... yes I know where that is... two o'clock... sure... okay. I will see you then. Goodbye Mr. Panzer." Handing the phone back to Blue, Woodson turned, and without so much as a word, walked back toward the lake.

"Who was that?" Blue inquired impatiently. "Who's Panzer?"

Woodson stood quietly by the water's edge. He didn't answer.

"Woody! Who is this Panzer guy?' she pressed on, now sounding very annoyed. "What does he want?"

Woodson turned back toward Blue and shot her a half smile. "Only the largest collector of Mayan artifacts in North America... It seems that he wants me!"

"Now what would he want with you?" inquired Blue suspiciously.

"I'm not exactly sure, but it sounded like he wants to hire me."

"To do what?"

"Consulting, more than likely," replied Woodson as he skipped a stone across the surface of the lake. "I'll find out tomorrow at two o'clock."

"Look Woody," began Blue while she waved an accusing finger, "You promised Lyons that you would take it easy—"

"Relax, Blue," Woodson tried to reassure her as he picked up another stone to skip across the lake. "I'm just going to talk to the man... he probably wants to ask me some questions about Gonzalo Guerrero. I'm sure that's all."

"Well I'm going with you." Blue continued to wave a menacing finger.

"Not this time, Blue." Woodson shook his head. "He just wants to see me."

"What the heck—?"

"Panzer wants a private meeting," he quickly interrupted. "Even if you come, I'm sure he'd have you wait in another room. From what I've heard, these collectors are supposed to be quite eccentric.

Blue dropped heavily into one of the chairs, and with both hands pulled her long brown hair away from her tanned face. "I just know you're going to get yourself into trouble. I just know it."

Woodson didn't answer. He just stared out over the water. The sun was beginning to set and the clouded sky shrouded the lake with many different shades of orange and pink. Woodson watched the sun slowly set making sure to conceal his smile from Blue.

"The Mr. Panzer," he said under his breath. "I think this is going to be very interesting!"

Also by Robert Bresloff

"...This first of a series to get young readers "into" the classics delivers a rip-roaring debut and presents a multidimensional avenue to introduce literature to a large audience, including reluctant readers..."

-School Library Journal
(for The Wee Musketeers)

The Wee Musketeers

ISBN: 978-0-9820812-5-9

Book 1 of the Get "Into" the Classics series

It was early 1960's and there wasn't much else for three eleven year old boys to do in the small town where they lived. Playing with wooden swords they would act out the novel, Bobby pretending to be Athos, Fritzy, Porthos and Keith, Aramis. Little did they know that very book that inspired their games, the one Grandpa Max read to them often, was indeed magic. Given to him by a mysterious old woman at a book sale. Bobby's Grandfather quickly discovered he could transport himself into the stories. Once Grandpa Max realized he had interfered with the plot, he summons Bobby and his friends to help him repair the damage. If they fail every copy of The Three Musketeers would change forever.

Robin and the Little Hoods

Book 2 of the Get "Into" the Classics series

Bobby and his friends team up with Grandpa Max again...this time in Sherwood Forest!

If you are interested in ordering any of theses titles you can order online at EATaBOOK.com or write the publisher:

Attn: Sales Department
Gauthier Publications
P.O. Box 806241
Saint Clair Shores, MI 48080